Hum Bear

Hum Bear

SARAH HOWARD

© Sarah Howard, 2017

Published by Sarah Howard

A CIP catalogue record for this book is available from the British Library.

ISBN 978-0-9955837-0-2

Book layout and design by Clare Brayshaw

Illustrations and cover design by Stuart Trotter

Prepared and printed by:

York Publishing Services Ltd
64 Hallfield Road
Layerthorpe
York YO31 7ZQ

Tel: 01904 431213

Website: www.yps-publishing.co.uk

With love to my Grandchildren
Lauren, Luke, Lillie-Grace, Anthony,
Anna-Sofia, Lenni, Zeb and Baby

ACKNOWLEDGEMENTS

Thanks to my husband Ken
for all his patience and support.

Many thanks to John Keable.

Also thank you to Stuart Trotter
for the illustrations.

A bridge, a bear
A gingerbread star
A bright pink balloon
And a Silvery Moon

Mix the old and the new
Tie a red ribbon too
Silently hush
Grows a leafy green bush

Add a girl called Amy
Is all you will need
For a wonderful story
For you to read.

PART ONE
Amy's Discovery

ONE

Amy was a very quiet, shy little girl who didn't talk very much. Maybe she wasn't a chatterbox but she always listened well and noticed all that was happening around her. Amy also did a lot of thinking and had a fantastic imagination. She lived with Aunty Jean and Uncle Rob in a big old house that was near the River Humber. The river had a huge bridge spanning over it called the Humber Bridge*. It was one of the largest single span suspension bridges in the world. Amy often looked out of her bedroom window at night. She could see the Humber Bridge and she often wondered what was over the other side.

There were also other children who lived in the big old house. Amy thought she was

* See page 194

~ 1 ~

different from the other children because she was so quiet. Amy would watch the other boys and girls play games, sing, dance, laugh and joke. Sometimes they could be very noisy and naughty. Sometimes the other children would tease Amy and call her names which would really upset her. Amy never said anything back to them, she wasn't that sort of a girl. Aunty Jean and Uncle Rob could become very cross and annoyed if the children misbehaved. But Aunty Jean and Uncle Rob were really very kind and Amy liked them; but they were just always so busy with the other noisy, naughty children.

Amy overheard the other children saying that Aunty Jean and Uncle Rob weren't their real aunty and uncle but their foster parents. Neither was the big old house their proper home, nor were they even a real family, but that they were all living in a foster care home.

Amy wasn't too sure what all this meant. She could remember happy days when she was a very small girl and did have a real family. Amy never knew her daddy; he had sailed away to sea before she was born and never returned. She remembered her mummy so well. She was very pretty with yellow hair, blue eyes and a beautiful smile. Mummy would tell her bedtime stories, hum tunes, sing songs and give her lots of cuddles.

Amy especially loved it when mummy baked gingerbread biscuits because Amy would help by cutting them out into star shapes. When they were baked, mummy would write everyone's name on them with white icing. Afterwards, Amy and mummy would take the gingerbread stars to Grandad Charlie and Granny Anne's house. They would eat the gingerbread stars with a glass of milk … mmm … they tasted scrummy, delicious.

At Christmas time, the gingerbread stars with the names iced upon them were made extra special. Granny Anne would sprinkle them with silver glitter and tie them to the Christmas tree with red satin ribbons tied into bows.

Amy loved to visit granny and grandad's house. There was much fun, laughter, singing and music there. Amy could remember it all so fondly.

Grandad Charlie was a captain of a ship. He had a thick grey beard and always wore his sea captain's hat. He had lots of tales to tell of his travels across the world, which would make Amy laugh; funny stories and jokes about him boxing with kangaroos and wrestling with crocodiles in Australia. He could also be wise and speak of a time when Hull was a busy port and many ships and trawlers sailed from there. Grandad Charlie would tell Amy about looking for signs in the sky.

"Red sky at night, sailor's delight. Red sky in the morning, sailor's warning." ... "What this means," explained Grandad Charlie, "is that if the evening sky looks red, it is a sign that the next day will be a good one. If the sky looks red in the morning, it is a sign of a bad weather." The sky over the River Humber could look quite glorious at times with its magnificent blazing red and orange sunsets.

He would talk of plans for the future when his sailing days were over and he would have enough money to buy a lovely new house were Amy could visit and stay. It would be near the river, where he could keep a small boat and in the garden there would be a swing and a big Wendy house where Amy could enjoy herself.

"When and where would it be?" Amy would ask her grandad excitedly.

"Don't you worry Amy. One day, there'll be a place of our own somewhere for us," Grandad Charlie would reply.

Granny Anne used to be a singer and she had a beautiful voice. Grandad Charlie would strum his guitar, and they would both sing songs together about a place for them *"Somewhere"*. But then everything changed. Mummy had to go away. Amy heard people talking about her mum having a problem, that she was very ill and had to go a long way away for a long time to get better. Grandad Charlie had gone far away sailing across the world on a big ship. Granny Anne had taken a very nasty fall and broken her hip, which would take a long time to mend. She had also bumped her head very hard in the fall, which made her lose her memory. Granny Anne did not even recognise Amy or Amy's mum, Susan. Granny Anne needed a lot of time and care to help her get better, so she needed to go and be looked after in a care home.

There was no one to take care of Amy, which is why she came to live with Aunty Jean and Uncle Rob and the other children in the big old house near the river.

TWO

One day it just rained and rained all day. Amy felt really sad and alone this day. She went to bed that night wishing for things to change. Well, at least the rain had stopped. There was a big, bright full moon that shone into Amy's bedroom. Amy peered out through her bedroom window and she saw the Humber Bridge. The Humber Bridge had a pair of very large towers which rose up high from the banks of the river. The bridge towers stood tall, black and proud, in front of an enormous white, round moon. The moonlight shone over the river, bathing it in light, causing the river flow to shimmer and glow. Amy gazed through the window for a while at this magnificent monument, when suddenly, something took Amy by surprise! ... There in the distance, Amy could see a shadowy shape.

Peeping out from behind from one of the bridge's dark black towers, appeared the shape of a little teddy bear. It was a small black silhouette against the silvery light of the big, round, full moon. Amy was spellbound. As she continued gazing, the little teddy bear appeared to wave to Amy. Amy's heart fluttered as she waved to the little teddy bear. The little teddy bear waved back.

The next day Amy wondered if it had all been a dream. But a few nights later, the same thing happened again. The shadow of the little teddy bear peeped out once again from behind the tall black towers of the Humber Bridge. This night, the moon was a slightly smaller crescent shape and the stars twinkled in the dark-grey night sky.

Amy was so happy at the sight of the little teddy bear appearing again and waving to her. "Oooh, it's the little Humber Bridge bear," she squealed out with delight to herself. Then suddenly, to Amy's amazement, the little teddy bear appeared to pluck one of the stars right out of the sky. Amy watched with excitement as silver glitter fell from the star. It sprinkling down like a silver shower by the side of the Humber Bridge. It reminded her of when Granny Anne sprinkled the gingerbread stars with silver glitter at Christmas time.

Amy awoke the next day, wondering again if it had all been another dream. She sat in her room pondering about it. Surely it couldn't have been another dream? After all, the shape of the moon had changed and many more stars had appeared in the night sky. Her thoughts were interrupted when she heard the other children scurrying down to breakfast.

Everyone ate their breakfast and then went outside to play. This day the sun was shining in the clear pale-blue sky. Amy could hear Aunty Jean calling, "Come along children, it's a lovely sunny day. We are all going for a walk along by the river."

The group of them set off for a nice long walk along the side of the river. Amy, as usual, walked quietly at the back of the group with her head hung down, her long, goldie-brown curls tousled down over her shoulders, her hands clasped together in front of her plain cream crumpled dress.

Uncle Rob was pointing to all the ships bobbing along the river; a smaller tug boat was pulling a larger boat. Amy's thoughts drifted to thinking of her grandad, far away across the sea on the other side of the world on his big ship. The other children were having fun throwing small pebbles into the water to see who could throw the furthest. But then Amy's eyes were drawn to the giant of a bridge, spanning over the river with its rows of traffic driving over it. The bridge's twin towers were looming high and loftily up towards the sky. Amy wondered what was on the other side of the bridge and if she would ever go across it. More importantly, what about the little teddy bear that she had seen waving to her in the moonlight?

The group of them walked on further along the river bank until they reached a playground and enjoyed time playing on the swings and slides. Afterwards, they played football and some ball games. All the fun of the morning gave them all quite an appetite. They sat out in the warm sunshine and ate a mouth-watering picnic. An ice-cream van passed nearby, pealing out some tuneful chimes. Chocolate, strawberry and vanilla ice cream cones with multi-coloured sprinkles were ordered. The children loved the ice creams, which were a rare treat for them. They tasted so yummy, cold and delicious. The perfect ending to their picnic on this beautiful summer's day.Later, when they were returning back home, Amy was lagging behind and couldn't keep up with the rest of the group. She was puffing and panting from the walk in the hot sun. Amy started to think again about the teddy bear she had seen the night before; she still could not decide whether it had all been a dream or not.

Suddenly, as she was walking along not far from the Humber Bridge, Amy stumbled. She fell over and grazed her knees. No one had noticed that Amy had fallen. 'OUCH!' she yelped, drawing in a sharp breath as she fell, stretching out her full length on the grass. Her knee really did sting. Amy sat up to give her knee a rub. Then, suddenly, Amy spotted something. There ... there right in front of her ... sat under a leafy green bush ... was a little teddy bear with a tiny glistening of silver glitter across one arm. For a moment, Amy was bewildered. She could hardly believe her eyes. Could this possibly be the same little teddy bear she had seen waving to her from the Humber Bridge? The pain of her grazed knee was disappearing fast. Quickly, she scooped up the teddy bear, tucked it over her shoulder and covered it with her long curly hair. The colour of the teddy bear's fur blended in well with Amy's own hair. No one noticed what was hidden under Amy's long tousled curls as she hurried along. She started to run as fast as she could to catch up with the others. She didn't want anyone questioning her about her precious new find. In the distance she could hear Aunty

Jean calling, "Hurry up children, we will be late home for dinner."

Amy could hardly contain her excitement as she arrived back at the old house. Somehow she knew she had just found something very special. Quickly she went upstairs and hid the teddy bear in her bedroom. Then, as quick as she could, she returned to join Aunty Jean, Uncle Rob and the other children for dinner.

Amy 'wolfed down' her dinner and was the first to finish her meal.

"Goodness Amy!" said Aunty Jean, surprised to see how fast Amy had eaten her food. "You'll give yourself indigestion, eating at that rate!"

"Sorry Aunty Jean, it's just that I was really hungry. All that running about near the river has given me quite an appetite. Can I go to my room now? I feel like I need to go to bed early. I am also really tired from all the running about by the river," said Amy with a big yawn.

"Very well," replied Aunty Jean.

Amy skipped off excitedly to her room. She couldn't wait to go and give her new-found discovery a closer inspection. She burst through her bedroom door and slammed it shut behind her. With an expectant smile upon her face, Amy was just about to seize up the teddy bear into her arms, when she heard Aunty Jean calling out.

"Amy, are you quite sure you are all right? You are behaving a bit oddly."

"No, really Aunty Jean, I'm fine, just a little tired," Amy insisted, as she hastily hid the teddy bear away under her pillows. Amy did not want anyone else to know what she had found.

"OK. Amy, but do let me know if you need anything, and PLEASE don't slam the door. I am going to be busy for a while now."

Amy was pleased Aunty Jean was going to be occupied, so she quickly got herself ready for bed and changed into her nightdress. Then she heard some of the other children making a lot of noise. Two of the boys were fighting. Aunty Jean and Uncle Rob were not very pleased to see one of the boys with a big black eye. Aunty Jean and Uncle Rob dealt with the boys and sent them both to bed.

Amy was just about to pick up the teddy bear when she heard a knock on the door. It was Sophie, one of the little girls who lived in the big old house.

"Amy, do you want to come and play in the garden with me for a little while before bedtime?" called out Sophie.

"No, sorry Sophie, I'm changed into my nightdress now and I am too tired to play anymore," replied Amy.

"OK, Amy, I'll see you tomorrow," Sophie called back.

Amy waited quietly in her room until everything had gone completely quiet. She did not want any further interruptions.

Later that evening, in the privacy of her room, Amy picked up the teddy bear from under her pillows and held him up in front of her eyes. Curiously, she stared into his face with wonderment. His fur was a goldie brown. The teddy bear's head was slightly tilted forward onto one side and he had large, rounded, pricked-up ears. He had big soft warm brown eyes and a cute little half smile spreading up onto the side of his face. He wore a navy blue waistcoat which had a pocket and two small brass buttons. The teddy bear was a little old and worn and had a yellow patch sewn with black thread upon the top of his shoulder. Even so, he was still very soft, furry and cuddly. Amy thought he was adorable.

Amy could not believe what she saw next ... the little teddy bear had something in his clasped paws. Amy looked closer. "What are you holding there?" she said curiously as she uncurled the teddy bear's paws. To her astonishment, the teddy bear was holding a gingerbread star with Amy's name written upon it!

"Oh gosh," Amy giggled in amazement. "Where on earth did you get that gingerbread star with my name on? … You really are a very special little bear. Now I must give you a name … But what can I call you?" said Amy, thinking out loud to herself.

"I know," she said, feeling pleased with her idea. "I found you near the Humber Bridge so you can be my little Hum Bear. Yes, I will call you Hum for short. I do hope you like your new name, Hum," said Amy, thinking out loud again as she spoke to the little teddy bear.

To Amy's further amazement the Hum Bear replied, "Mmm … mmm".

Amy chuckled. "Ooh you really are a proper little Hum Bear!"

Then the Hum Bear did something even more extraordinary and amazing. He kept humming and humming more and more and then lifted himself up and started to circle in the air around Amy's room. He whirled round and round like a helicopter and spun and hummed like a spinning top. Then he glided down gently back into Amy's arms.

"Wow! Magic! You are awesome!" shrieked Amy. Then Amy stopped and paused to think. She was a little concerned. "Now that I have found you, Hum, I don't want to lose you. I had better not tell anyone just how very special you are or someone may try to steal you away from me."

Hum Bear replied with a "Mmm … mmm".

Amy gave another giggle. She hadn't giggled or chuckled in such a long time and it felt good. At this moment, Amy caught sight of herself in the dressing table mirror and she noticed that her usual sad expression was disappearing. Amy stood there staring at the reflection of herself holding the Hum Bear. Amy raised her head, lifted her chin up and gave a broad smile.

"I think things are going to be much better now I have found you to talk to and I won't be so sad and lonely any more," Amy told the Hum Bear.

"Mmm … mmm," replied Hum.

THREE

Over the next few weeks, a strong bond grew between Amy and Hum. Amy would sit in her room with Hum and tell him all her troubles; about how different she felt from the other children because she was so quiet and shy; how much it upset her being teased and called names. Hum would just look back at Amy with his ears pricked up as though he was really listening to every word she had said. Hum looked at Amy with his big soft brown eyes as though he really cared. The kindly half-smile on the side of Hum's face never changed. Amy knew that Hum would never call her nasty names. Hum was like the best friend any little girl could hope to have. Each night before going to bed she would tell Hum all about her sadness, and Hum would just nod his head and keep softly replying

"Mmm … mmm". Amy felt much better having her new-found friend to talk to. Amy would then say, "Come on Hum, snuggle close to my tum" and then she would cuddle the Hum Bear and fall, contently, fast asleep.

As the weeks passed by, Amy was becoming much happier and more talkative. She joined in activities with the other children and all the teasing and name-calling stopped.

However, something was really bothering Amy and one night before bedtime, she told Hum what it was. "Oh Hum, I do miss my mum," she wept. "Will I see her again? Is everything going to be all right?"

Hum just kept replying, "Mmm … mmm".

A huge tear welled up in Amy's eye, it trickled down her cheek and fell with a splash onto the Hum Bear's chest. The tear drop absorbed right through Hum's little waistcoat and into his soft fur. This must have stirred something in Hum, for Amy could not believe her ears or eyes for what she heard and saw next. In the silence of her room, she heard a very gentle sound: pe-pum, pe-pum. It was the sound of a heartbeat. For a few seconds, the shape of a golden heart shone out from the Hum Bear's chest; glowing and fading with the rhythm of the beat. Then Hum started very, very softly to hum a tune.

Amy was absolutely stunned. She picked Hum up and held him close to her ear to listen as carefully as she could. Then, Amy recognised the tune. She remembered it ... she knew it ... the tune that Hum was humming!

"The tune is from the song that granny and grandad used to sing about a place somewhere!" Amy exclaimed excitedly.

The memories of the song came flooding back to her. She hadn't heard it for so long. Oh she knew it, oh she knew it so well. In her mind's eye she could recall her Granny Anne singing of a place 'Somewhere' and her Grandad Charlie strumming his guitar.

The lovely melody soothed away Amy's heartache. Amy could recall every word of the song that Granny Anne and Grandad Charlie used to sing. Her spirits were so joyfully lifted and she began to sing her grandparents' song. Amy sang and sang and sang her heart out. Her voice was beautiful and crystal clear.

Aunty Jean and some of the other children could hear a beautiful voice. They wondered who it was singing and came running to Amy's room. "Oh Amy, you have the voice of an angel," remarked Aunty Jean. The other children cheered and clapped. Amy felt so, so happy, her sadness was melting away. Everyone was so impressed with Amy's lovely voice, they paid very little attention to the Hum Bear held in her arms. But at least now she didn't have to hide him any more.

"Amy you're a smashin' singer," piped up a little boy named Jack, who spoke with a very strong Hull accent. "I've heard that ther's gonna be a fella on the telly soon called Sam Bowell who turns children who are good singers into stars."

Amy was too shy to think about going on television. She was just happy about the Hum Bear and that everyone liked her singing. Then, all of a sudden, her confidence took a sudden dip.

"Well!" said a girl named Hayley, stomping her foot and tossing her head back with a haughty air. Standing with her hands on her hips, Hayley spoke to Amy in a sneering manner and went on to say, "I think it is a stupid song! And far too old fashioned!"

At first Amy felt deflated and crestfallen by Hayley's harsh criticism. Then with a sudden spur of new found courage she replied.

"Well, even if you don't like it and think it is old fashioned, I really like this song because it brings back happy memories for me and reminds me of real people who really loved me and that is what is important," said Amy, tossing her head back boldly.

"Yeah," a boy named John-Paul chipped in. "My dad was from Liverpool and he was always singing a song about never walking alone and having hope in your heart."

"I like that," said Amy. "Songs and music make you feel good and you should always have hope in your heart."

Hayley was thinking about what the others were saying ... "Perhaps you're right," she said slowly and a little more humbly. "Everyone should have hope, especially kids like us who are in Care."

"Yeah, it's not our fault we are in Care," said John-Paul.

A sweet little singing voice from a little girl named Sophie chirped out from amongst the group. "When the red, red robin comes bob, bob bobbin' along ..." she sang, shaking her head from side to side. "I remember! I remember!" she recalled excitedly. "My dad loved rugby. He was a Rovers' fan and he used to sing the Hull Kingston Rovers*' supporters' song." ... Sophie smiled, remembering her dad singing that old sweet song.

Another little boy named Billy shouted out excitedly, "My mum was a rugby supporter too but she liked the black-and-whites rugby, Hull

* See page 196

FC*." Billy started to sing their supporters' song, "Old Faithful, we'll roam the range together, Old Faithful, in any kind of weather", and Billy smiled, remembering that his mum used to sing that great rugby song.

"Hull City, Hull City. Up the Tigers*," chanted two football-mad older boys named Kenny and Chris, as they thrust their fists up into the air and let out a loud cheer.

Aunty Jean and Uncle Rob had been stood together quietly, watching and listening to the children. They both kept looking back and forth at the children and then to one another, both with huge grins on their faces.

"Who'd have thought such a quiet girl like Amy would have such a stunning voice," whispered Aunty Jean to Uncle Rob,

"Yes," replied Uncle Rob, "and just look at the effect she is having on all the other children. I have never seem them so happy and friendly with one another."

"Phew," they both said together, breathing a sigh of relief.

* See page 196

FOUR

Over the next few weeks, Amy was singing a lot and her lovely voice could be heard all around the house. The other children were often joining in the singing too. The mood in the house had lifted and all of the children were much better behaved.

One day, Aunty Jean was sitting in the front room. She was holding her chin in her hand as she was pondering and becoming increasingly curious about the change in Amy. Aunty Jean was concerned that Amy was growing too big to be spending so much time carrying a teddy bear about with her. Aunty Jean didn't know how extraordinary the Hum Bear was and how he had helped Amy to find her fantastic, singing voice. Later that afternoon, Aunty Jean had a long chat with Amy.

Aunty Jean started asking Amy questions about where the Hum Bear came from. At first Amy was reluctant to say where she had found the Hum Bear. Finally, Aunty Jean coaxed the truth out of Amy about her finding him under a leafy green bush near the Humber Bridge. But Amy did not expect what Aunty Jean was to say next.

"Amy, it doesn't belong to you. You must return it, someone may be looking for it."

"No! No! Please, please, Aunty Jean, don't make me lose my special little friend," Amy pleaded and pleaded with her. But Amy's pleas were all in vain. Aunty Jean insisted that she took the Hum Bear back to where she had found him. Aunty Jean stared firm and hard, right into Amy's eyes. Amy felt that Aunty Jean's stare was so fierce it was enough to turn Amy into stone. Amy knew that when Aunty Jean insisted something had to be done she was not to be disobeyed. However, Aunty Jean agreed for Amy to keep the Hum Bear for one last night.

That evening in her room, a tearful Amy spoke to the Hum Bear. She told him that she did not want to send him back, that she loved him and that she would miss him so, so much. Amy talked and talked and talked to the Hum Bear, until eventually she realised perhaps Aunty Jean was right, that Hum didn't belong to her and she had to let him go.

"I'll return you to the place where I found you near to the leafy green bush near the Humber Bridge tomorrow Hum," Amy told him reluctantly.

Hum replied, "Mmm ...mmm". At least this reply reassured Amy a little that she was doing the right thing.

Amy looked out of her bedroom window and stared at the Humber Bridge. This night there was no bright, full moon but a magnificent brilliant-red sunset. The night sky was ablaze with burning colours of red and orange and pinks set behind the Humber Bridge. A large flock of starlings swarmed, swooped and swirled, looking very small and black in contrast to the bright evening sky. Amy suddenly remembered what Grandad Charlie had told her, that a red sky at night was a good sign, that the next day would be a good one. Amy knew that Grandad Charlie was old and wise and knew many, many things and always spoke the truth. Amy trusted that her parting with Hum was not going to be as difficult as she thought.

The next morning, it was a lovely sunny day when Amy took Hum back to the spot where she had found him under the leafy green bush.

But first she had lots and lots of questions to ask him.

"Did you find me for a reason, Hum?"

'Was it to help me find my voice and happiness?"

"Will I be happy without you?"

"Are you going to find who it is who you belong to?"

"Are you going to help someone else, like you have helped me?"

To all her questions, Hum replied and nodded with an enthusiastic "mmm ... mmm".

All of this made her separation a little easier.

Amy had one more question for the Hum Bear.

"Are you going to find another little boy or girl like me?"

But Hum remained silent. Hum always stayed silent when the answer was no, and this puzzled Amy.

Amy knew it was now time to say goodbye. So she kissed Hum tenderly on the forehead as she sat him down under the leafy green bush. "Goodbye Hum. I will never forget you. I love you right up as high as the moon and stars in the sky and more. I hope we will meet again someday soon. I hope you will find whoever you belong to and that they will take good care of you," she said, crying tearfully as she gave Hum one last great big hug. She started to walk away slowly and gave Hum one last wave. Hum waved back to Amy.

Amy turned around and ran swiftly back to the big old house as fast as her little legs could carry her. Her hot tears were streaming down her face and slightly stinging on her cheeks. By the time she had arrived back home, she was feeling very, very angry with Aunty Jean. Amy stood before the front door of the big old house and paused to take a deep breath, before boldly bursting through the door. She stomped down the hallway and went into the back room where Aunty Jean was sitting in an armchair. Amy's face was flushed and she was out of breath from running so fast. She wiped the tears from her face with the back of her hand and stood before Aunty Jean, shaking and trembling.

Amy scrunched up her face, looked directly at Aunty Jean and started to shout at her.

"You made me give Hum back because you said he didn't belong to me. I hate you!" she yelled angrily at Aunty Jean. "Well, I don't belong to you so give me back to my mum!" demanded Amy, hardly able to get her words out she was so angry, upset and breathless.

"Sit down Amy," said Aunty Jean firmly. "I have something to tell you. It's good news." Amy immediately started to settle down and was "all ears" waiting to hear what this good news could be.

"Your mum is much better now. She has a new house on the other side of the river. Go and collect your things. I'm taking you to give you back to your mum."Amy's jaw dropped, her mouth wide open in amazement, she was so stunned and speechless by this happy news. Amy thought this was turning out to be a good day after all. Perhaps Grandad Charlie was correct about the red sky being a good sign.

Amy could hardly pack her suitcase fast enough, she was so excited. Amy had a quick check around her room making sure she hadn't left anything. She opened her dressing table drawer and there was the gingerbread star that Amy had found in the Hum Bear's paw. Amy was distracted by Aunty Jean who was calling, "Are you ready yet Amy? Hurry up, the children are waiting to say goodbye to you." Dashing about, Amy popped the gingerbread star into her cardigan pocket. Uncle Rob was waiting outside her room to carry her bags downstairs.

Amy came downstairs where all the children were waiting in the hallway. The children said their goodbyes and told Amy how much they would miss her and that they were sorry for all the nasty names they used to call her. Amy told them that she would miss them and that she was glad that they had all become friends.

"We'll remember to keep hope in our heart," said John-Paul. "Oh yes, do that," said Amy. "I know things have been very difficult for you all, but you are a great set of kids really; not bad, just sad, and I hope everything works out well for you all," said Amy, speaking quite grown up for her young years.

"Before you go Amy, we have something for you," said Hayley, pulling out a book. "We didn't have much time but we have all signed this book for you."

Amy opened the book and, inside, the children had cut out some golden stars and stuck them into the book and written their names on them. Amy told them that she would always treasure the book and remember that their names were written in the stars.

"Goodbye Amy. Miss you," said all the children chanting and waving altogether.

"Goodbye. Miss you more," replied Amy, waving back as she climbed into Aunty Jean's car, sad to leave her friends but looking forward to seeing her mum again.

Aunty Jean drove the car over the Humber Bridge. Amy felt very high up as she looked out of the car window and saw tiny-looking boats sailing along down the river below. After they had crossed the bridge, Aunty Jean drove up a street and parked the car near a small house. A lady appeared at the door. She walked down the path carrying a very large pink balloon tied with a long red ribbon. "Yes, yes it's mummy!" squealed Amy, jumping for joy with delight. They both ran to each other. Mummy picked Amy up and swung her around in her arms, but as she did so the large pink balloon blew away.

"I'll leave you now," said Aunty Jean. Amy and mummy said goodbye to Aunty Jean and thanked her for taking good care of Amy.

"Oh, how you have grown Amy," mummy remarked. "The pink balloon was part of your welcome home gift, but come see what else I have for you." Mummy took Amy into the back garden and there, propped against the wall, was a bright shiny new bicycle. "This is for you to ride when we go to visit people."

"Oh thank you mummy," said Amy, "but who will we be visiting?"

"Ah, you'll have to wait and see, but right now I have something else to show you," said mummy, taking hold of Amy's hand and leading her upstairs. Opening a door, mummy said to Amy, "This is your room. Do you like it?" Amy didn't like it, she loved it! It was all decorated in pink, which was Amy's favourite colour. Next to the bed was a wooden rocking chair. Sat upon the rocking chair was a cuddly silvery-white teddy bear with a red satin ribbon tied in a bow around its neck. It reminded Amy of the colour of Granny Anne's glossy silvery-white hair. The red satin ribbon reminded her of Granny Anne tying the gingerbread stars onto the Christmas tree.

That evening, Amy sat snuggled up with mummy, her new teddy bear and a mug of hot chocolate. "Are you going to give your new teddy bear a name?" inquired mummy. Amy thought about it, but first she decided to tell mummy all about the Hum Bear and how she came to name him after the Humber Bridge. Mummy was amazed by Amy's story, but so happy that Amy had found the little Hum Bear to help her while she wasn't there.

Then, as a thought suddenly struck her, Amy said, "I know what I am going to call my new teddy bear." Because my other bear was called Hum and I had to cross over the Humber Bridge to be with you, I am going to call my new teddy ... Bridget."

"Oh yes," agreed mummy. "Mmm ... yes ... Bridget Bear. Yes, I like that name."

Mummy paused for a while, thinking hard about something she had just remembered, and then said to Amy, "I have something else to show you." Amy's mum took an old photograph album out from the cupboard. "Look at this photograph." Amy stared at the old black and white photograph. It was of a young girl with long curls that looked a lot like her. "That girl looks a lot like me," remarked Amy with a puzzled look upon her face, "but I know it is not me because she is wearing a ribbon tied in a bow in her hair and I have only ever worn an Alice band in my hair, never a ribbon bow."

"No it's not you Amy, but you really do look like this girl," said mummy with a smile. "It's your Granny Anne when she was a little girl about the same age as you."

Amy studied the photograph of the little girl who was sat near a small green bush. Then she spotted something that made her gulp and almost choke on her hot chocolate with surprise. There, sat next to the girl, was a little teddy bear, with his ears pricked up, big eyes and a half smile on the side of his face. His paws were clasped together. He had a patch upon the top of his arm, too. Amy held the photograph up nearer to her face to take a closer look.

"Mummy, do you have a magnifying glass?" she asked.

Mummy had one in the drawer and gave it to Amy. Amy held the magnifying glass over the photograph and peered through it. Amy's eyes grew larger in astonishment. She could see what the teddy bear was holding. It was a gingerbread star! There was no mistaking that this was the same bear as Amy's Hum Bear.

"Oh," gasped Amy, realising what she had just seen. "My Hum Bear must have belonged to Granny Anne when she was a little girl."

"I think you could be right about that," said mummy, who was as equally surprised as Amy. "Your Granny Anne did mention something about having a very special little teddy bear which she used to sing with when she was a child, but I don't know the full story. I wonder what has happened to the little bear over all these years?"

"Maybe he was whisked away in a time machine or has been helping others in care homes like me?" suggested Amy, with a little giggle.

"Who knows," said mummy shrugging her shoulders. "Anyway, enough excitement for one day, it's getting past your bedtime."

"OK, mum," said Amy, sleepily rubbing her eyes. Off to bed she went to sleep in her new pink bedroom. She could hear the pitter-patter of raindrops on her bedroom window becoming louder and louder. It felt so cosy and warm in her new comfy bed, snuggled up with Bridget. "Oh Bridget, I do like you, but I really do miss my little Hum Bear," she said wearily as she drifted off to sleep.

FIVE

During the night, a very heavy storm brewed up. Amy was woken up suddenly by a loud clap of thunder and a bolt of lightning which gave a flash of light right across her bedroom. It gave Amy quite a scare. She jumped out of bed in fright and scooped up Bridget before flopping into the rocking chair. Amy rocked to and fro, squeezing Bridget tightly. At first Amy was afraid of the thunder and lightning. "I'm frightened," she said, whispering to Bridget softly. Amy was in for another surprise, but quite a pleasant one. Suddenly, Bridget stretched out her long soft furry arms, wrapped them around Amy and gave her a great big cuddle. "Oooh," said Amy in shock. "Now I have another special little bear. Bridget you are my little Hug Bear!" Amy started to feel calmer and the storm calmed also. Amy climbed back into bed and was soon fast asleep again.

Next morning Amy wondered if she had been dreaming about Bridget's cuddle. Mummy mentioned that there had been a very heavy storm the night before. so Amy knew at least that much was true.

"What are you going to do today, Amy?" asked mummy.

"It's still raining a little, so I will stay in my room and play with Bridget until the rain clears," answered Amy.

Back in her room, Amy picked up Bridget. The rain was slowing down until finally it stopped. The hot sun's rays had come out and were drying up all the rainfall. A long ray of sunshine, which appeared to have a long pointed golden finger upon the end of it, streamed in through Amy's bedroom window. Then this light stream, with its long golden finger, gently stroked Amy's face. Then the golden pointed finger of the light stream started to bend and curl. It beckoned to her as it eased its way backwards through the window. Beckoned by this warm sun ray, Amy walked to the window and looked out of it. She could see the clear blue sky and there was a brilliant arc of bright colours; it was a magnificent rainbow.

"Look Bridget, there's a rainbow and there's the Humber Bridge too!" said Amy pointing up to the sky. Then … something else caught Amy's eye. Blowing in the breeze was Amy's welcome home gift. The bright pink balloon with the red ribbon still attached to it was swirling about in the breeze. Amy gazed after the balloon. It was heading in the direction of the Humber Bridge. As the balloon reached the bridge, it stopped at one of the tall towers. At first Amy thought that the balloon had disappeared and she felt a little disappointed because it had gone. But then, no, the balloon had not gone. It reappeared from behind the tall tower. Amy gasped, for there was something she recognised. There, floating through the sky, holding tightly onto the balloon's red ribbon. It was the Hum Bear!"Look, look Bridget, its Hum!" Amy exclaimed, hardly able to contain her excitement. "But what on earth is he doing?"

Suddenly Amy felt Bridget tapping her pocket. "What is it Bridget? Are you trying to tell me something?"

Amy felt inside her pocket. She had forgotten that she had put her gingerbread star there before she left the old house. Amy pulled it out of her pocket and looked at it. She stared at the writing in disbelief because it didn't say Amy …

the name written there on the star in white icing sugar was Anne! Amy was thinking and thinking and looking and looking, making doubly certain she had read the name correctly. Then she realised who the Hum Bear was going to help. Of course, of course, she thought, it wasn't another little boy or girl, it was her Granny Anne! Amy called out from the window excitedly, "Go, Hum, go! Go find my Granny Anne and help her to remember."Amy started to feel a buzzing sensation in her ears, followed by a humming sound and a new song in her heart.

Amy started to sing in her beautiful angelic crystal-clear voice:

"The rain has gone,

Now I have a new song.

It's here in my heart,

Waiting to start,

To sing out loud

Far over that cloud.

Over the rainbow in the sky

My voice will soar and sing on high."

Amy's voice "took wings" and soared out of her bedroom window, up through the clear blue sky, over the rainbow, over the Humber Bridge, over the rooftops, carried off onto the breeze to follow after the Hum Bear.

The Hum Bear was being transported through the sky by the balloon in the breeze. He started flying faster and faster, sailing through the air over the River Humber in the direction of Hull. Then, oh no, it was starting to become very windy. Hum was heading towards a very, very tall building. It was a hospital, the Hull Royal Infirmary. A sudden gust of wind was blowing Hum nearer and nearer to the tall hospital building. He was on a collision course, about to crash into the hospital.

Suddenly, another gust of wind had picked up the breeze that was carrying Amy's airborne voice. Amy's voice continued singing and was growing stronger and stronger, chasing faster and faster after Hum. The "singing wind" wrapped itself invisibly around Hum, and snatched him out of danger. It was just in the nick of time and Hum managed to change direction. Hum was whipped up and around as though he was almost dancing in mid air. He sprinkled a small amount of silver glitter dust that landed upon a window pane. It settled like magical star dust, sparkling and glittering in the sunshine on the hospital window.

A poorly little boy in hospital was watching in awe, hardly believing his own eyes, as to what he had just seen happen. "Oh wow! See him go!"

he shouted out. "A singing teddy bear holding a big pink balloon just flew past and sprinkled some star dust on the window!" The little boy gained a pink rosy glow in his pale white cheeks and he started to feel much better.

The Hum Bear was back on course, steering the balloon in the right direction over Anlaby Road. Amy's voice still continued singing and urging Hum to "Go find Granny Anne". But the voice was losing its puff. The wind was becoming much lighter and Hum was dropping down and beginning to fall towards the ground. He was heading towards a crash landing into Hull City football club's playing field. Fortunately Hull City was playing a match and had just scored a winning goal. The crowd erupted, going wild, cheering and gave out an almighty tiger's roar. The strength of the noise of those City fans was so powerful it rose up, causing enough wind to carry the Hum Bear and Amy's voice upon their way again.

The wind started picking up quite strong and fast. It became very windy and it was blowing Hum, with the balloon and Amy's voice, all over the place. The red ribbon was wriggling and shaking about like a snake in the sky. Hum was just managing to hold on tightly when, suddenly, there in the sky, flying towards Hum in mid air, was a giant green and yellow toad kite. The red ribbon that Hum was holding and the dangly green and yellow bows hanging from the toad kite suddenly became tangled up and Hum couldn't fly. Hum and the toad kite were just hovering and spinning helplessly up in the air with the wind blowing around them.

There was a boy flying the kite. It was John-Paul, with all the children from the big old house. John-Paul tried to reel the kite in but it wouldn't move.

"Look," shouted Hayley pointing her finger upwards. "There's Amy's teddy bear and I can hear Amy's voice too, but I can't see Amy."

"What is she saying?" asked John-Paul.

"She's calling out, 'GO HUM GO! GO FIND MY GRANNY ANNE'," Hayley told him, repeating Amy's words.

"It must be something very important. We have got to help free the Hum Bear from the toad kite somehow so that he can go and find Amy's gran. But how are we going to do it?" said John-Paul.

Suddenly, Sophie began to sing in her cute little voice. "When the red, red robin comes bob, bob, bobbin' along, along, There'll be no more sobbin' when he starts throbbin' his old sweet song."

All the children's heads turned around, staring in surprise at Sophie.

"Sophie, this is no time to start singing a song," Hayley told her sternly. "We have to find a way to free the Hum Bear."

"Wait!" Sophie replied excitedly. "Look!" And she pointed her finger up to the sky. Suddenly, a little robin redbreast appeared from nowhere and flew over to where Hum was tangled up with the toad kite.

The little bird pecked and pecked and pulled and pulled away at the tangled ribbons until Hum and the toad kite finally became separated. All the children cheered and clapped, shouting out "Go Hum go! Go find Granny Anne", their voices lending support to Amy's voice and urging the Hum Bear along his way.

Sophie was so pleased and happy too. Every time she sang the Rover's song, a little robin redbreast had started to fly near her. He was a lovely little bird and had become a very helpful little friend to Sophie, so she decided to give the little robin a name and she named him Craven.

"Go Craven go! Go help the Hum Bear find Amy's Gran," Sophie cried out to him.

The Hum Bear, still holding tightly to the balloon, was on his way once more. He breezed along on the crest of an airwave, Amy's voice still blowing, singing and urging after him in the wind. Craven was flying and swooping ahead, on the lookout to help the Hum Bear find Granny Anne.

SIX

Meanwhile, a thin-framed old lady, with glossy silver hair and a sleepy head, was sat with a nurse on a garden bench. It was Granny Anne, sitting out in a beautiful fragranced flower garden of a care home. A butterfly fluttered by and then Craven, the little robin, flew down and parked himself on the fence. He sat there, merrily chirping and tweeting his own sweet song.

"Oh that song has woken me up!" said Granny Anne in surprise, as she caught sight of the little robin redbreast sitting there singing on the fence. "A robin. I remember my dad was a red-and-white rugby supporter. They were known as the Robins. My Charlie was a black-and-white rugby supporter!" She chuckled as she remembered the rivalry and banter between her father and her husband.

The nurse was stunned by what Granny Anne had told her, but was very pleased that Granny Anne's memory was returning. The nurse was also amused to hear about the rivalry and banter between Granny Anne's father and husband. Hull was a great rugby town with two great teams and often a lot of competition between the supporters which, at times, could be quite serious. And sometimes quite funny.

At the bottom of the garden some bees were buzzing around the purple and blue flowers.

"I can hear humming," said Granny Anne to the nurse, as she cupped her hand around her ear to listen more carefully.

"It will be the sound of the bees you can hear. They are very attracted to the purple and blue flowers," replied the nurse.

"No, this is definitely a humming sound that is a different sound from the buzzing of the bees," said Granny Anne, listening very, very carefully. "And oh, what else do I hear? A beautiful voice that sounds like an angel singing!"

Just as Granny Anne was speaking, the Hum Bear, still holding the balloon, glided down and landed gently on the bench next to Granny Anne. Amy's angelic voice had helped Hum find her Granny Anne but now it faded into a whisper and blew away in the breeze.

"Why, what have we got here?" exclaimed Granny Anne as she took the balloon and tied the dangling red ribbon to the arm of the garden bench to stop it from blowing away. As she was tying the ribbon, it gave Granny Anne's memory a jolt.

"I remember a long time ago tying gingerbread stars to the Christmas tree with red satin ribbons like this one," she told the nurse.

Granny Anne picked up the Hum Bear and stared at him intently. "I used to have a teddy bear like this one when I was a little girl. He was called Bertie Bear and he helped me learn how to sing," she told the nurse. The nurse smiled back warmly at Granny Anne, but not really believing what she was saying.

Granny Anne kept staring and staring at the Hum Bear and memories were being unlocked in her mind. "Why, I am sure this is my teddy bear I had when I was a little girl. I called him Bertie. He has that same yellow patch sewn with black cotton upon his shoulder. When I was a little girl, an older girl with long ginger hair, called Meg, was jealous of my singing. She used to bully me and call me nasty names. One day, Meg tried to snatch Bertie away from me, but I wouldn't let go. However Bertie had a big rip on his shoulder where his arm was nearly torn off. My mother used a scrap of yellow material and stitched it on with black cotton to try and repair it," Granny Anne told the nurse. "See, it's still there after all these years," she said, pointing to the yellow patch at the top of the Hum Bear's arm.

The nurse was amazed at what Granny Anne could remember and how much she was talking. Granny Anne was normally very sad, quiet and not very talkative.

Then Granny Anne noticed something in the Hum Bear's paw. It was a gingerbread star ... and there was a name written upon it. Granny Anne took the star out of his paw and held it up to read it. Written upon the star in white icing was the name, Amy.

"Amy," said Granny Anne softly, reading out loud. She went on to say to the nurse, "Amy. Of course, that's my grand daughter's name. We used to write names on gingerbread stars in white icing. I need to go and find Amy, and my daughter Susan, who is Amy's mum."

At that moment another nurse came into the garden to let Granny Anne know that she had a visitor waiting for her in the lounge. Granny Anne walked into the lounge holding the Hum Bear. A man with a thick grey beard and wearing a sea captain's hat stood there. "Is that really you, Charlie? I thought you had forgotten me," said Granny Anne.

It was Grandad Charlie. He had returned from his voyage that had taken him sailing around the world.

"I could never forget you, Anne. I am sorry I have been away so long but I could not abandon my ship or my men. I have earned enough money now to buy our dream home," said Grandad Charlie, his eyes filling up with tears.

Granny Anne held up the Hum Bear. "Charlie," she said "we need to go and find Amy, I want to give her this teddy bear."

"Don't worry Anne," replied Grandad Charlie. "Amy is safe with her mum. They are both well. You'll see them soon, I promise, but first we have to make some preparations."

SEVEN

The following week, Amy was at home baking gingerbread stars with mummy. When they had finished, mummy told Amy they were going for a bicycle ride. Mummy took the gingerbread stars, wrapped them up and placed them in the saddle bag of her bicycle.

"Where are we going?" asked Amy. "You'll see soon," replied mummy.

"Can Bridget come too? I could put her in the front basket on my bike," said Amy.

"Of course she can," mummy replied.

Off they went cycling down the lane. Amy could see across some fields which were like patchwork quilts. The two of them rode on around a twisty bend and came to a row of houses. The house at the top had a signpost near it that read, "SOMEWHERE PLACE". Mummy took Amy through the garden around to the back of the house, and there she saw a swing hanging from a large apple tree and a Wendy house that Grandad Charlie had spoken of. Amy sat Bridget down inside the Wendy house. Then she ran excitedly into the house, expecting to see her grandparents there. But the house was empty.

"Mummy, is this the "place somewhere" that Granny and Grandad used to sing about? And where are they?" asked Amy.

"Wait," replied mummy. "I have something else to show you. Just keep listening and looking carefully."

Mummy took Amy by the hand to the bottom of the garden and led her through a gate. There she saw a boardwalk leading to a small stream with a jetty. Amy listened and looked carefully but all she could hear was the distant quacking of ducks in the Wetlands and a flock of birds flying overhead. Then there was just silence. Amy looked down the stream and saw nothing; hardly a ripple in the water, nothing but mist in the distance. Amy kept looking and listening and then she saw and heard something. Sailing out of the mist was a small boat and, in it, there was Grandad Charlie strumming his guitar. Beside him was Granny Anne holding the Hum Bear. Amy could hear the Hum Bear humming and

Granny and Grandad singing their song about a place somewhere.

The small boat sailed closer and closer. Amy was jumping up and down unable to hold her excitement and she ran towards her grandparents.

Granny and Grandad climbed out of the boat. They all laughed and hugged each other, being overjoyed about being together once again.

"Amy, I have something for you," said Granny Anne. "This teddy bear once belonged to me when I was about your age. Now I would like you to have him."

"Oh thank you, Granny Anne, thank you so much. I can't tell you how much he means to me," replied Amy, happily jumping for joy again.

Amy took Hum and Bridget to look inside her new Wendy house. There was a small bed, a table and a chair inside. Mummy had put some of the gingerbread dough on the little table. With a little toy rolling pin and shape cutters, Amy cut out some gingerbread stars for mummy to bake in the oven.

Afterwards, they all sat together again, eating the delicious yummy gingerbread stars, with their names iced upon them, with a glass of milk. It was just like they had done all those years ago.

Afterwards Grandad Charlie suggested that they all have a photograph together at their new home.

"Can Hum and Bridget be in the photo as well?" asked Amy.

"Of course," replied Granny Anne, starting to remember more and more. "I lost my teddy bear when I was a girl whilst I was distracted having my photograph taken. I was all dressed up in my best clothes and my hair tied in a red ribbon bow. My father told me to put my teddy bear down to one side by a green bush. It was near the River Humber before the Humber Bridge had even been built. After I had been photographed, my father, who was a very good singer, started to sing his favourite song to me. It was called "Scarlet Ribbons". That is why I have always loved red ribbons. Anyway, we were both singing and a group of people gathered around to listen. They enjoyed our singing and they all clapped and cheered. They talked with us for a little while, but after they had gone, I could not find my Bertie Bear anywhere. I searched and searched but he was nowhere to be found. I was so upset. All those years I never saw him, but somehow I always knew I would see him again some day.

"Well," said Grandad Charlie, "the teddy bears are staying with us and being part of our lives. We will take a photograph of us all to make brand new memories." And he promptly took off his sea captain's hat and placed it upon the Hum Bear's head. Amy could not stop laughing at Hum in her grandad's hat.

They all had a lovely family photograph to treasure outside their new house with the street sign, Somewhere Place.

That night, Amy went to bed happy and content. She had her beloved Hum Bear back. Amy placed Hum and Bridget together on the little wooden rocking chair. Before climbing into bed, she kissed them both goodnight.

"Goodnight, my wonderful hummable Hum Bear. Goodnight, my lovely huggable Bridget Bear," she said to them in a very sleepy voice.

"Goodnight Amy. Time to switch the light off now," called mummy through the open bedroom door.

In Amy's dimmed room, the moonlight shone though the bedroom window like a spotlight shining over Hum and Bridget who were sitting comfortably on the rocking chair. The rocking chair started to rock gently to and fro. Suddenly, Bridget stretched out her long, soft, furry arms and wrapped them tightly around Hum and gave him a great big snuggly cuddle. For a few seconds, in the silence of Amy's room, the gentle sound of a heartbeat could just be heard, "pu-pum, pu-pum". His golden heart shone out from his little navy blue waistcoat, glowing and fading with the rhythm of the beat. "Mmm ... mmm," went the Hum Bear in his usual way. The half-smile on his face stretched up towards his eye and he gave a cheeky wink.

Goodnight ... then all was silent. Amy was tucked up nice and cosy in her warm bed, falling fast asleep and dreaming of what could have happened to Hum before she had found him under the leafy green bush.

PART TWO
New friends at
Somewhere Place

ONE

During the night, Amy was slumbering soundly, far away in the land of nod. She was dreaming about the Hum Bear. In her dream she was asking the Hum Bear who had taken him away from the spot where Granny Anne had placed him, all those years ago, near the leafy green bush. The Hum Bear showed her two gingerbread stars with the words 'Meg' and 'How' written upon them. Then she saw a room full of books, clocks, a few teddies and some drawings of horses, dogs and birds. In her dream, a telephone started to ring, but then Amy woke up. She rubbed her eyes, stretched out her arms and looked over to where Hum and Bridget were sitting on the rocking chair. Amy smiled happily at the two furry bears and climbed out of her cosy bed. She picked up her two precious bears and sat in the rocking chair, cradling them both in her arms.

"I've just had a very strange dream," said Amy, yawning sleepily. "It was quite a nice dream really, but I don't think the dream was about a place I have ever visited before, but somehow the bears looked very familiar."

But the dream was soon forgotten as mummy was calling Amy to get ready for school.

Amy had started a new school and mummy had a new job. Mummy loved cooking and baking and she had gone to work as a cook at the care home that had cared for Granny Anne. Amy had settled well into her new school. Her favourite subject was reading and she loved playing the recorder with her new friend Lillie. Amy and Lillie always sat together in class and became the very best of school friends. They both practised very hard at their recorders and soon both of them could play very well. Every night when Amy was back in her room, she would still continue to talk with the Hum Bear, telling him how her day had been. Amy would also practice her recorder at home, playing tunes to Hum and Bridget, sitting them in front of her, rather like they were her audience.

It was now the long hot summer holidays; no school for six whole weeks (yippee!). Amy was being looked after every day by Granny Anne and Grandad Charlie at their home, Somewhere Place, while mummy was at work.

One day Grandad Charlie had been out all day. Later, he arrived back home with a big grin on his face. He had a surprise present for Granny Anne. It was a little black-and-white dog. Grandad Charlie had put a red plastic rose in the little dog's collar. Granny Anne was delighted with the puppy.

"Shall we call her Rosie?" said Granny Anne, taking the red rose from the puppy's collar. But Grandad Charlie didn't like that name.

"No," he said firmly. "This dog is like a black-and-white faithful sheepdog and I want her to be called Faithful. It also reminds me of the words of my favourite Rugby team, Hull FC's song, *Old Faithful.*"

"Oh no," protested Granny Anne. "I think Rosie is a much better name and I much prefer red and white to black and white."

Amy stood there with her arms folded, chuckling to herself about her grandparents disagreement over the puppy dog's name. "Adults!" she thought to herself, rolling her eyes. Amy thought the dog actually looked rather peculiar. It had the hugest pair of ears she had ever seen and a really odd-shaped face that made her look more like a miniature black-and-white cow than a sheepdog.

"What about calling her Daisy?" suggested Amy, secretly feeling amused.

"Daisy? Oh, no way do we want her to be called Daisy. It sounds more like a cow's name," retorted Granny Anne and Grandad Charlie together in agreement.

"It's settled then," said Grandad Charlie. "This dog is going to be called Faithful. I am sure that faithful to us she will be."

Amy stared at the dog with her strange looking face and very large ears, but there was something so appealing about this dog that Amy found her to be quite adorable.

Faithful started running round and round the garden. She then crouched down with her front paws stretched out flat on the grass, just the way a real sheepdog does when rounding up the sheep. This little dog was becoming more and more amusing and made Amy giggle. Suddenly, Faithful jumped up onto the garden wall. The little black-and-white dog walked along the garden wall, her huge ears sticking out from the sides of her head, balancing like an acrobat. Suddenly, she then leapt off the wall. Grandad Charlie was calling for her, "Faithful, Faithful". He had some dog treats and her lead ready to take her for a walk. Faithful was so excited she ran swiftly to Grandad Charlie and leapt up and licked his face. She was remarkably strong and agile for such a young dog and she almost knocked poor Grandad off his feet.

"Steady on girl. I feel as though I have just been rugby tackled," said Grandad Charlie, both shaken and amused at the same time. "We had better take you for a long walk. You need plenty of exercise."

Grandad Charlie put Faithful's lead on her and took her off for a long walk.

Amy could hear children's voices giggling over the other side of the wall. She overheard them saying, "That dog is so funny she should be in the circus!"

They had been watching Faithful's antics as she tried to walk and balance along the wall.

Amy wondered who was speaking, so she walked over towards the wall. She then saw a set of fingers curling over the top. Then another set. Another and another, until there were two sets of hands curling over the top of the wall. Then she saw two heads with two shocks of bright-red flame-coloured hair pop up above the wall. Each head had a long ponytail on the side. One on the left side of the head and the other one on the right side of the red head. Then two girls' faces appeared, with two pairs of bright green eyes, two freckled noses and two wide, grinning mouths.

"Hi. We're Megan and Gemma. We are identical twins."

"What's your name?" asked the girls in unison.

"Hello. My name is Amy," she said, introducing herself. "Have you come to live in the house next door?" she asked.

" Yes," replied Megan. "We've just moved in with our Aunty Pat and Uncle Jeff."

"And our brothers too," added Gemma.

Just then, a tall dark-skinned boy with short, dark, curly hair appeared. His arms where strapped across his puffed out chest and his shoulders were pulled back. He stared at Amy. His face looked very unfriendly. He walked off without speaking.

"That's our brother Wilber," said Gemma.

"Your brother!" said Amy in surprise. "You don't look a bit alike; not like you two, who look exactly the same."

"Wilber is our half-brother. We have same mum but we have a different dad," explained Megan. "Wilber doesn't talk very much. Aunty Pat says that he needs to be given time because he's been through a very difficult time."

"He's a great brother really," continued Gemma. "He's very tough. We used to live in a very rough neighbourhood but Wilber looked after us and wouldn't let anyone pick on us or bully us. He's really clever too. He always gets A grades in maths."

"Uncle Jeff calls Wilber 'iron man' because he is so strong and tough. He also says that Wilber will be quite a 'force to reckon with' when he grows up," added Megan.

Wilber walked back over to where the girls where standing. "I like Uncle Jeff," he said bluntly. "He plays football with me and my brother. When I grow up I want to be an electrician, just like Uncle Jeff."

The girls turned around, surprised to hear their normally quiet, solemn, surly brother having so much more to say. Just then, another boy's face appeared next to the twins. He had sandy coloured hair, blue eyes and a very cheeky looking face.

"This is our other brother, KC," the twins told Amy.

"KC? That's an unusual name. I've never heard anyone called that before," said Amy, looking puzzled.

"Well, his real name is Kenneth Charles, but everyone just calls him by his initials, KC," explained Megan. "And he is a right chatterbox," added Gemma. "Aunty Pat says he will be a very good communicator when he grows up."

"I like Aunty Pat, she's really nice, but I want to be a bus driver when I grow up," said KC. "That is if my legs get better."

KC had been in hospital recently. What nobody knew was that he was the little boy who had seen the Hum Bear "fly past" the hospital window and scatter silver glitter onto it.

Amy was beginning to wonder why these children all looked so different and were living with an aunty and uncle and not their parents. She started to think of her time in the big old house and all the other children living with Aunty Jean and Uncle Rob. Perhaps these children were also in foster care, like she used to be.

The twins and KC started chattering away, telling Amy all about how much better it was now, living with Aunty Pat and Uncle Jeff rather than with their mum. That now they weren't cold and hungry and frightened like they were before. They had had no friends before because other children wouldn't play with them because their clothes were dirty smelly and ragged. Now they had nice clean clothes to wear and clean warm comfy beds to sleep in and plenty of nice tasty food to eat and toys to play with.

Suddenly, Wilber started to shout at his brother and sisters.

"Shut up! Be quiet!" He snapped at them. "It's nobody else's business! We are very lucky not to have been split up. It was very good of Aunty Pat and Uncle Jeff to take us all together as a family. We have to be careful not to let anyone split us up again. And we definitely don't want to go back to our mum's house. It stinks and all those horrible nasty people who used to stay there were awful. We hated it there and we never want to go back!"

"It's OK," said Amy softly. "I know what it's like to be in foster care, but now I am very happy to be back home with my mum. She is at work now. This is my grandparents' house. They look after me while she is at work."

Wilber, Megan, Gemma and KC looked back at Amy in surprise. They didn't expect Amy to tell them that. All the other children at school lived with their parents. They didn't know any other children who had foster parents.

"Will you be our friend?" asked KC.

"Yes, of course. I'd love to be your friend," replied Amy. "You can come over into my garden and play on my swing and in my Wendy house, if the grown-ups allow us to."

"No thanks, that's cissy!" was Wilber's blunt reply.

"Oh yes, yes!" squealed the girls excitedly. "We'd love to play in your Wendy house."

"Can I have a go on your swing," asked KC, with a longing in his voice. "I have never been on a swing before."

"Yes, of course you can," replied Amy, finding it hard to believe a young boy had never been on a swing. She had been to the park many times with her mum and played on the swings.

The twins were very energetic and came into Amy's garden jumping, dancing and doing cartwheels. Then Amy heard a clip-clop noise that sounded like horse's hooves on the pavement. KC wandered in after the girls. To Amy's surprise, KC had long metal rods on his legs and there was also metal attached to his shoes which was what was making the clip-clop noise on the footpath.

"Why do you wear those metal rods on your legs?" asked Amy curiously.

"They are called calipers," replied KC. "I have a problem with my leg and hip. I have to wear the calipers for two years until my hip and leg are stronger. By then everything should be all right. The calipers are quite heavy and rub against my skin which makes my legs sore, but it's what needs to be done to help make my legs get better."

Amy noticed how small KC was. The raised calipers just made him look much taller than he actually was.

"C'mon KC," said Amy. "We'll all help you with the swing."

Megan and Gemma each took hold of one of KC's hands and helped him onto the swing that was hanging from the apple tree. Amy gently pushed the swing and KC rocked to and fro. He was really enjoying himself, and was laughing out loud. It was good for him to play out in the fresh air and have fun after his long stay in the hospital.

Next, they all went into the Wendy house. It was furnished with a doll's cot and a small table and chairs. Sat upon the chairs were Bridget and the Hum Bear. Gemma went over and picked up Bridget and stroked her long, soft, glossy silver fur. Then Megan joined her sister and gave Bridget's fur a stroke. Then, much to the twins' surprise, Bridget stretched out her arms and wrapped them around them both and gave them a great big cuddly hug. The twins giggled and squealed with delight.

Then KC spotted the Hum Bear. He was amazed. "It's the bear! It's the bear! The one I saw with the pink balloon; the one that I saw fly past the hospital window. The one that left the silver glitter on the window," blurted out KC as he pointed excitedly to the Hum Bear.

Nobody but Amy heard the Hum Bear softly murmuring "mmm … mmm" in his usual way. But Amy knew that what KC was saying must be the truth because no one else would have known about the pink balloon.

Megan and Gemma started to chatter away, telling Amy about how poorly KC had been in hospital and how much he had improved after seeing and hearing a singing teddy bear pass by the hospital window, holding onto a big pink balloon. KC really started to like teddy bears after that. He really wanted to have a teddy bear of his very own.

Then he met a kind lady, called Mrs Estuary, who owned a bookshop. She used to come to the hospital and read stories to the poorly children. When she heard about KC and that he had never had a teddy bear of his own, she brought him a pair of sandy coloured musical teddy bears. One teddy played a drum and the other played the banjo. KC had named them Bart Bear and Bo-Jo Bear. He loved playing with those teddy bears so much that Mrs Estuary let him keep Bart and Bo-Jo after he left hospital. He now kept both the bears in his bedroom at Aunty Pat's and Uncle Jeff's house.

TWO

Amy's mum came home from work and was pleased to see Amy playing happily in the Wendy house with her new friends. Mummy had baked some gingerbread star biscuits and asked the children if they would like to have their names iced upon them. "Ooh, yes please," said all the children together. The smell of fresh, baked, yummy, delicious gingerbread filled the air, making the children's mouths water.

Mummy couldn't write Megan's and Gemma's full names on the gingerbread stars so she shortened them to Meg and Gem. The twins and KC were delighted. They all sat together staring at the iced gingerbread stars which looked very, very tempting but also looked almost too good to eat. Then Gemma noticed something about their names.

"Look," she said. "Our names are like a reflection of each other; g-e-m spells meg backwards."

"Oh, yes it does," said Megan in surprise, "and m-e-g spells gem backwards too."

Amy was staring at the gingerbread stars, particularly the one with the name Meg written upon it.

Megan was about to take a bite of the gingerbread when Amy suddenly shouted out, "STOP!" She had suddenly remembered the strange dream she had had the other night when the Hum Bear had shown her a gingerbread star with the name "Meg" written upon it. Amy was very puzzled about this.

"Megan, have you ever seen the Hum Bear before today?" asked Amy.

"No, never," replied Megan truthfully. She was quite puzzled by Amy's question.

"Do you know anyone else by the name of Meg?" asked Amy, still puzzled.

"No, I don't think so," came back Megan's reply.

Then Gemma butted in. "What about old Aunt Meg after whom we were named? Don't you remember the story about how we come to get our names?"

"Oh yes, that's right," said Megan, as she started to remember.

Then they both recalled the story that their mum had once told them about how they were given their names.

When they were born, their dad had left them all, and their mum had no money. When old Aunt Meg heard about their situation, she sent money to their mum to buy clothes, nappies, cots and a twin pram. Old Aunt Meg had earned and saved money from travelling around the country, working as a dancer. Later she was married to old Uncle Jim, who was a deep sea fisherman, but they never had any children of their own. Old Aunt Meg was very pleased to hear that they were twin girls and would always have each other as sisters. The twins also knew that they had inherited the same flame-red hair colour as old Aunt Meg and their mum. At first, the twin's mum didn't know what names to give the baby girls so she called them her little baby redheads. Then the twin's mum was so thankful for old Aunt Meg's kind gift that she decided to name one twin in honour of her. That twin was Megan. The other twin was like a little bright gem, so she was named Gemma. The baby twins was so much alike they looked like mirror images of each other.

Amy was very interested to hear the twins' story, but was still puzzled about her dream and the gingerbread star with the name Meg written on it. She wondered what it could mean and hoped that perhaps one day she would find out.

A voice called out from over the fence. It was Aunty Pat calling for Gemma, Megan and KC. It was time for them to go home.

That evening, Amy was sitting with her mum, enjoying a mug of hot chocolate before bedtime. She was thinking about the earlier conversation she had had with the twins, which had made her think about her own dad. Mummy had never ever spoken about him and Amy wondered if he had left them, like the twins' dad had left them. So she decided to ask her mum if her dad had just left them also. Mummy was quite shocked by Amy's question.

"Oh, no, no!" said mummy in horror. "We need to talk Amy, so that you understand clearly what happened to your father. What you have heard from the twins about their family situation is very sad, but ours is an entirely different story."

Mummy explained to Amy that her dad was a fisherman. He was looking forward very much to Amy being born, but he was lost at sea just weeks before her birth.

"I know he would have been very proud of you and a wonderful father too. I was heartbroken to have lost him. His name was Jamie. Before he went off to sea, we had already chosen your name. We decided to call you Amy because it sounded similar to Jamie," said Amy's mum. She went on to tell Amy, "Your dad would have done anything he could to have made us happy. If he could, he would have given us the moon and the stars. He also loved it when I made gingerbread stars, just like you do."

"Did you write daddy's name on the gingerbread?" asked Amy.

"No," replied Amy's mum. "There wasn't enough room to write his full name Jamie, so I just put on a blob of jam instead," she laughed.

Amy laughed too.

"Oh, you do sound like your dad when you laugh," her mum told her.

"Well, in that case I will laugh more often," said Amy, laughing some more.

Amy went on to tell her mum of the night when she first saw the Hum Bear wave to her from behind the Humber Bridge. She described it as a moonlit, starry night and that there was something so magical about the silver stardust that fell from the star that Hum had appeared to pluck from that starry night sky.

"Er, er … Amy," said mummy, pausing. Then, choosing her words carefully, not really wanting to spoil the illusion, she went on to say, "The moon doesn't shine directly behind the Humber Bridge in the way that you have described. The moon would have been positioned differently and much, much higher in the dark night sky."

"But anyway, that's enough chatter for one night," said mummy awkwardly, wanting to change the subject. "You are looking very tired. It's getting past your bedtime."

Amy went off to bed. She snuggled down into her cosy bed and cuddled the Hum Bear.

"But, who knows ..." Amy thought to herself in wonderment. "Perhaps in some way my dad did bring and show the moon and the stars to me that night I first saw the Hum Bear."Amy drifted off and was soon sound asleep. Soon she was dreaming about the Hum Bear showing her gingerbread stars, with the names MEG and HOW written upon them.

THREE

The next day, Amy was back playing in the garden at Somewhere Place. Granny Anne and Grandad Charlie had become friendly with their new neighbours, Aunty Pat and Uncle Jeff. They were talking over the garden wall. Faithful was running round and round the garden, performing her usual funny antics, much to everyone's amusement. Aunty Pat asked how the little black-and-white dog came to have such an unusual name. Grandad Charlie told them it was because of his love for Hull FC rugby team and the supporter's song *Old Faithful*. Uncle Jeff told him that both he and Aunty Pat were keen Hull FC supporters too. The grown-ups discovered that they all shared some of the same interests, rugby and football. They were all very keen Hull City (The Tigers) football fans.

While the grown-ups were busy chatting, the children were also getting to know each other better. Amy's school friend, Lillie, had also come along to play and had brought her recorder with her. Amy brought out her recorder too. KC was showing off his two battery-operated musical bears. Bart Bear tapped up and down on the little drum with a pair of little drum sticks. Bo-jo Bear gently strummed the banjo. Wilber was standing in the background, watching. The twins were their usual energetic selves, cartwheeling, dancing and jigging about all around the garden.

"Wilber has some bongo drums," said KC, "and he can play them really well."

Wilber frowned and remained silent. He just continued to stay quietly in the background, not looking very happy. He was quite a hard tough boy who found it difficult to be sociable because he was not accepted. In the rough neighbourhood where he used to live, the other children would not play with him because of the dark colour of his skin. Nobody really took the opportunity to get to know him. He was really a very nice lad.

"I wish I could play a musical instrument. I would love to be able to play something like a banjo or guitar," piped up KC.

"My grandad knows how to play the guitar. Perhaps he might teach you how to play," said Amy.

Grandad Charlie overheard them talking. "Of course I'll teach you how to play the guitar," he said. He went indoors and came out carrying two guitars, and handed one to KC.

"Oh, cool. Thanks so much," said KC, taking the guitar excitedly.

Everyone sat out in the warm sunshine while Grandad Charlie gave KC his first lesson. KC was a very quick learner and was thoroughly enjoying learning how to play the guitar.

Amy and Lillie started playing their recorders. Wilber was still watching, but his face was starting to look less serious. He started to tap his foot slightly. Then he suddenly walked off. He returned a few minutes later carrying his bongo drums. He sat down with everyone else and started to beat the drums. He banged away at them and played them really well. Everyone clapped him and Wilber's sad face turned into a beaming smile.

"Can we have a concert?" asked Megan.

"Ooh, yes, yes. What a good idea," said Gemma gleefully. "And can we pretend that all the bears are the audience?"

The children collected up the bears and sat them in a row on the grass. Everyone else took up their places on the wooden decked area, eager to play their instruments together. Just as they were about to start their music practice, the Hum Bear toppled over. Amy went and picked him up. As she did so, he started to hum a tune into Amy's ear. Amy listened carefully and then, as she walked back to pick up her recorder, he started to hum the tune out loud, "m m m m m m m … la la la la lal la lal la laa".Amy copied Hum and also started to hum the tune.

Amy's little tune caught Grandad Charlie's attention. He looked up in surprise saying, "I know that tune. It is called 'Dueling Banjos'.""Can you teach us how to play it?" asked KC enthusiastically.

"Of course I will," replied Grandad Charlie, pleased with the children's enthusiasm.

With Grandad Charlie's skill and patience and all the children's eagerness, they were soon making a wonderful sound of blended music. Even the twins, who did not have a musical instrument, put on their tap shoes and tapped to the rhythm of the beat. Amy and Lillie played the tune on their recorders as a duo, followed by Grandad Charlie and KC playing the tune on their guitars. Next the twins tapped out the tune's rhythm with their feet in perfect unison, in the style of Irish dancers. Lastly, Wilber played the rhythm on his bongo drums. The group played and tapped softly at first. Then it became more competitive, growing louder and louder, building into a crescendo until Wilber was really banging out a mighty powerful sound on his drums.

Granny Anne, Uncle Jeff and Aunty Pat had heard the music and wondered where it was coming from. They could hardly believe how well everyone could play. The three of them clapped and applauded loudly.

"Well done, well done. That was really very good," said Granny Anne, still clapping her hands.

The children looked at one another and beamed. Even Wilber still had a smile on his face.

Suddenly, Faithful, who was indoors, started to bark very loudly. Granny Anne brought her into the garden but she still continued to bark loudly. Suddenly, a horse's neighing sound could be heard, then a girl's voice was calling out for Lillie.

"Oh it's my big sister, Lauren, riding her horse, Ruby. My father has sent her to take me home. Lauren lets me ride back on Ruby while she walks by her side and leads her with the reins," explained Lillie. "Come on over and I will introduce you to Lauren and Ruby."

All the children walked over to where Lauren and Ruby were standing. They stared curiously at the well-groomed, glossy, dark-brown horse with a purple head collar. Ruby was a very good-natured horse and didn't mind at all when the children fed her apples and patted and stroked her soft, smooth neck and mane. Even Faithful ran over to take a good look at another four-legged animal. She ran around on the grass playfully, stopping and stretching out her front legs, then having another run and letting out a few joyful "woofs" of excitement. Ruby appeared to be responding well to all the attention she was being given, and neighed and whinnied happily. Lauren told the other children that Ruby was a well-trained and very well-behaved horse, but they had to be careful not to stand too close to her back legs in case she might suddenly kick out.

"Well, it's time for us to go now, Lillie," Lauren told her young sister. "Dad's cooking tea tonight and he doesn't like us to be late. Mum will be home from work soon and our brother Luke will be back from his boxing training."

"Oh yes, we better be off home quick then," replied Lillie. "Luke's always starving when he's been doing his boxing and he eats everything."

Lauren helped Lillie to put on a riding hat for safety. Then she gave her a leg up to help her climb up to sit on to Ruby's back. Once Lillie was safely mounted in the saddle and Lauren had a tight hold of the reins, the horse trotted off. All the children waved. Amy remembered it would be her birthday the next week and she would be having a birthday celebration. She called out to them, "I'm having a birthday party next week. You are both invited and you can bring Ruby too."

"Oh yes, we'd love to," called back Lillie.

"Thanks Amy. I would love to bring Ruby too," added Lauren keenly.

That night, Amy lay on her bed stroking the Hum Bear. She was lost in thought, thinking of the lovely day she had spent with family, friends and animals. She thought of how much they had all enjoyed themselves and the fun they had had playing and making wonderful music together. Amy also cast her mind back to her other friends, John-Paul, Billy, Kenny, Chris, Hayley, Jack and Sophie who she had been in foster care with at the "big old house" whom she hadn't seen for quite some time. She wondered how all these other children were doing.

"I know," she said, thinking out loud to herself, "Next week, when it is my birthday, I think I will also invite the children I was in care with at the "big, old house" All my new friends can meet my old friends. We could go and have a big birthday picnic together on the grassy area near the leafy green bush, like I did the day when I found you, Hum."

"What do you think to that idea then, Hum?" Amy asked the Hum Bear.

"Mmm ... mmm," was Hum's keen reply.

"We could bring along Bridget, Bart and Bo-Jo for a teddy bear's picnic too. I think everyone would like that," said Amy, becoming increasingly excited.

"Mmm ... mmm ... mmmmmmmmmmm," replied Hum, even more keenly.

FOUR

It was the following week and Amy's ninth birthday had arrived. Everything was arranged and organised for all of Amy's friends to meet up on the grassy area near the leafy green bush not far from the Humber Bridge. It was a beautiful sunny day, just like the one when Amy first found Hum. Amy, Lillie, Wilber, Megan, Gemma and KC were sitting on a picnic blanket with their musical instruments, all eagerly waiting for the other guests to arrive. Hum, Bridget, Bart and Bo-Jo where also sitting in a row on the blanket near the children. Lauren was riding Ruby up and down the field. Faithful was running along by their side. The horse and dog really loved running about with each other.

Grandad Charlie, Granny Anne, Mummy, Aunty Pat and Uncle Jeff were taking all the delicious food out of the large picnic hamper ready for everyone to tuck into a tasty feast. Mummy had baked lots and lots of gingerbread stars and a big birthday cake with a picture of the Hum Bear on the top.

Lillie had given Amy a new recorder for a birthday present. The other children gave Amy a new rucksack. She was delighted with her presents. She decided to test out her new recorder and started to play a simple tune she had learnt at school. Suddenly, as she tooted out the tune, Amy heard a tweeting and chirping sound. She looked up and saw a small bird swooping about in the air above them. It was Craven, Sophie's little robin redbreast friend. Then, in the distance, Amy could just about make out some shapes of a group of people walking towards them. As they drew closer, she recognised who they were. First she could see Uncle Rob, followed by John-Paul, Jack, Billy, Kenny, Chris, Hayley and Sophie.Sophie was happily singing away, "*When the red, red robin comes bob bob bobbin along.*"

Amy jumped up and down with excitement at the sight of her old friends again.

"Great to see you all," Amy cried out. "But where is Aunty Jean?"

No one answered but they all stood giggling. Then Amy heard a buzzing and a rattling sound.

Next, she saw a great big giant bumblebee. It was Aunty Jean, dressed up in a black and yellow bee costume. She was shaking a collection tin in her hand and was collecting money for charity.

"Hello Amy. Happy Birthday," said Aunty Jean, giving Amy a kiss.

"Happy Birthday, Amy," chanted everyone else together.

Amy introduced all her old and new friends to each other. Soon everyone was having a brilliant time; playing games, eating the delicious picnic, and Lauren let the children take horse rides on Ruby.

"Let's get this party going," shouted out Grandad Charlie, strumming his guitar.

Carrying his guitar, KC tottered over to join him. Amy and Lillie sat with their recorders close to their mouths ready to blow into them. Wilber was there with his bongo drums at the ready. Megan and Gemma could hardly keep their tappy toes still, they were so eager to start dancing. They had all been practising hard to put on a fantastic performance for family and friends.

And then they began, starting out with a soft rhythm, which grew louder and louder and then exploding into a fantastic musical feast. Everyone thoroughly enjoyed the performance, clapping and applauding loudly.

Amy was becoming very hot, her long brown, curly, tousled hair was sticking to her face. "Come here, Amy. I will tie your hair back like Lauren and Lillie's braided hairstyle," said Granny Anne, pulling a scarlet red ribbon out of her pocket. Granny Anne started to brush and braid Amy's hair. Then she tied it back with the red ribbon in a neat bow. As she did so, Granny Anne broke out into an old song about scarlet ribbons. Amy joined in and they both sang a harmonious duo. Their voices were so beautiful everyone stood and listened in stunned silence.

"That was lovely. We've missed your singing at the big, old house Amy," said John-Paul.

"Well, maybe we should get together more often and enjoy songs and music," replied Amy.

"This reminds me of the time when I sang that song with my father all those years ago, just before I lost my Bertie Bear. (Bertie Bear was the name Granny Anne had called her bear before it became Amy's bear and she named it Hum.) It was in this same area many, many years ago, near to a green bush," said Granny Anne, remembering fondly.

Mummy came walking up with Amy's birthday cake, alit with nine candles. Everyone sang "Happy Birthday" and Amy blew out the candles on her cake.

"Make a wish, make a wish," called out KC.

Amy looked down at a picture of the Hum Bear on her birthday cake. She closed her eyes tightly and made her wish. Amy's wish was to find out what had happened to the Hum Bear back in the time he was Granny Anne's Bertie Bear, all those years ago when she had placed him near the green bush while she was singing with her father.

"What did you wish for, Amy?" asked Gemma.

"Oh, I can't tell you that," said Amy, "or else my wish won't come true!"

"We better start packing up now, Amy," said mummy. "Here's some leftover gingerbread stars. Put them in your rucksack with your recorder."

"Time to go already? Oh how time flies when you are having so much fun," said Amy as she put her new rucksack on her back, not wanting this wonderful time to end.

"Can we please play a little while longer?" begged Megan, clasping her hands together.

"Please, please?" added Gemma, also clasping her hands..

"OK then," said mummy. "Another ten minutes while we clear up."

Amy looked over to the leafy green bush. Lauren had tethered Ruby to it. Faithful was lying on the ground next to Ruby and Craven was flying about, circling above them. Then Amy spotted Grandad Charlie talking to a very, very old man who was standing next to the leafy green bush holding a sketch book. He looked much older than Grandad Charlie. The old man had very fine, greyish, wispy hair. He had a huge lump at the top of his nose which spread out, almost covering the whole of his left eye. The old man started drawing pictures in his sketch book. Amy wondered how the old man managed to see anything, let alone draw pictures.

Amy was curious and walked over to Grandad Charlie.

"Who is that old man? And what is he doing?" whispered Amy inquisitively.

"Oh, that's Art Robbie. I haven't seen him for many years. He was an old pal of my father's, your great grandad," explained Grandad Charlie. "He was a lovely old chap."

"Art Robbie? Is that his real name? And what about that lump upon his face?" asked Amy, still very curious to know more and more.

"Well, his real name is Arthur Robinson and he was quite a budding artist when he was a young man. That is how he came to be known as Art Robbie. He was in the Home Guard during the war and his lump was caused by a piece of shrapnel sticking in his face during a bomb blast. Art Robbie knows lots of stories of the brave people of Hull when many parts of their City were destroyed in the air raids."

"What are air raids?" asked Amy.

"It was when lots of bombs were dropped and exploded and many streets and homes were blown up. Many buildings were destroyed and left in piles of ruins on the ground. Hull was very badly bombed during the war and many lives and homes were lost. It was shattering but people from this area are proud and strong and have worked hard together to rebuild shattered lives. We must never forget that many, many brave people fought hard and gave their lives so that we may be free and have a better future," said Grandad Charlie with pride.

Amy gulped. "Oh, I never realised all that had happened!" said Amy, quite shocked at what she had just learnt. "I think we will learn about the war at school soon."

Suddenly a voice interrupted their conversation. "Finished!" It was Art Robbie. He had asked Grandad Charlie earlier if he could draw a picture of Ruby, Faithful and Craven near the leafy green bush. Art Robbie only drew pictures of animals, birds and plants. He hobbled over to where Amy and her grandad was standing talking and showed them the sketch he had just drawn.

Amy noticed that, because Art Robbie couldn't see very well, that the sketch of Ruby, Faithful and Craven near the leafy green bush had a hazy blurred outline. Nonetheless, the whole picture was very good and lifelike. Amy and Grandad Charlie really liked the picture. Grandad Charlie asked Art Robbie what he was going to do with it. Art Robbie told him that he was going to add the finishing touches to it at home, by adding some colour. With his paints, he would colour in the sketch of Craven with a red breast. He would paint in Ruby with a purple head collar and give her a nice dark-brown glossy coat. He would make sure that Faithful's picture had all the black and white markings exactly where they should be.

Art Robbie lived not far away. His home was next door to some friends, Eric and Eileen Estuary, who owned a bookshop. He used one of their rooms behind the shop as an art studio.

Amy seemed to recognise the name Eileen Estuary. She was a bit puzzled at first, racking her brains, trying to remember. Then she realised who she was.

"Ah, of course, I remember now. She was the kind lady KC told me about. The lady who read stories to him in the hospital. The same lady who brought him Bart and Bo-Jo, the musical bears," said Amy, muttering to herself.

"What are you muttering about, Amy?" Grandad Charlie asked her.

"Oh, nothing grandad. I'm just talking to my Hum Bear," replied Amy dreamily, as she was thinking about some ideas.

"Well, time is moving on, we'll have to be getting home soon," Grandad Charlie told her.

But Amy had other ideas. She was going to do something that she should never, ever do. Something very dangerous that children must not do. Never ever go off on your own without telling a grown-up you know where you are going. Amy was going to do something very naughty – sneak away and follow Art Robbie to the bookshop. She knew that next week it would be her friend Lillie's birthday and Amy thought it would be a nice idea to get her a book for a birthday present. Amy also knew that Grandad Charlie's and Granny Anne's wedding anniversary was approaching and they would love a drawing of Faithful to hang in their hall at Somewhere Place.

Amy's head was full of ideas about buying Lillie a good reading book. Thoughts of her birthday wish had gone completely out of her mind. But there was much more in store for Amy. Much, much more than she could ever have imagined.

Ruby, Faithful and Craven gathered together near the leafy green bush. Ruby and Faithful were standing there quite still and unusually silent. Craven perched himself quietly on a twig of the leafy green bush. He was not making any of his usual chirping sounds. All three of them were unusually quiet, sensing that something very, very extraordinary was about to happen.

ONE

Amy put on her rucksack containing her recorder and the gingerbread stars on to her back. She scooped up the Hum Bear tightly into her arms.

"This shouldn't take too long. We can go quickly and find a birthday present for Lillie. Nobody will notice that we have gone, they are all too busy clearing up after the party," whispered Amy into the Hum Bear's ear.

While no one was looking, Amy sneaked quietly away and followed Art Robbie. She was watching carefully and, from the distance, she saw him go into a bookshop. Amy approached the bookshop and, as she drew closer, she saw a big sign outside above the door which read:

Eric & Eileen Estuary's Bookshop

Amy was very lucky that she had found a good place that was welcoming to children. But this could have been a very different story; she could have met someone who was wicked and cruel to children.

Amy walked through the door and looked around at the hundreds of books, neatly stacked upon the many shelves that lined the bookshop's walls. Her eyes scanned over the books searching for that special one for a present for her friend Lillie. "Yes!" Amy thought to herself. This was just the right sort of place to find what she was looking for. This wouldn't take too long, there's bound to be something here that Lillie would like.

Amy was wandering around the large shop picking up books and glancing through them trying to find the perfect book for her friend. Just as she was walking near the back of the shop, she noticed another room. On the door was a sign that read:

Mr Estuary's Office.

Below this sign was a notice that read

Time Out. Keep Out.

Amy thought to herself, "how strange". She peeped into the room and she saw lots of different types of clocks, all of which were set at different times.

There was also something that Amy had never seen before. It was like some sort of computerised machinery with a large control panel displaying lots of buttons and switches. What Amy did not know was that this was a time machine. A man stood near the machine pressing some buttons. Then the telephone rang. The man, who was Mr Estuary, answered the telephone. Amy overheard him say, "Don't worry, we will have you back in no time."

Mr Estuary strode out of the room, taking long striding steps with his very long legs. Amy looked up at this very tall, thin man who wore very thick dark-rimmed spectacles. He had a very high forehead, shaped like a very large egg. His head appeared to have grown up and out through the sides of his dark hair that lay smoothly over and above his ears. He had a thick, dark moustache under his large nose. Amy could not help but try to conceal a smile to herself at the sight of this rather odd-looking tall, thin man. Mr Estuary was very, very intelligent. Not only did he own the bookshop, he also knew a lot about computers and TIME TRAVEL.

Mr Estuary looked down at Amy and smiled. He asked her if she needed any help. Amy told him that she was looking for a special book for her friend Lillie's birthday present.

"Eileen, can you come and help this little girl find a book for her friend?" called Mr Estuary to his wife. A plump, kindly looking lady walked into the room. She smiled and took a good look at Amy.

"Come this way. I've got the perfect book for you," said Mrs Estuary to Amy, leading her through to another room. Amy started to follow Mrs Estuary when she heard something making a sound. Amy's ears pricked up. It sounded like a "gong" or a "bong". It repeated five times, then stopped. "What's that sound?" she asked Mrs Estuary, with a puzzled look upon her face.

"It's the sound of the old antique grandfather clock which has a swinging pendulum. Every hour the clock chimes out the time. What you just heard was the clock striking five o'clock."

Then they walked through to the next room. Hum started to wriggle about excitedly, making his "mmm ... mmm" sounds. Amy was very surprised to see a group of teddy bears placed near some seats. She walked over to take a good look at them. She was even more surprised to see how similar the larger bear looked to Hum. It had the same goldie-coloured fur, the same soft brown eyes and the same half smile on the side of its face. This bear was a little larger and chubbier than Hum and wore a bright yellow checked skirt and a matching bow on its head.

"This bear does look like you, Hum!" said Amy to the Hum Bear. To which the Hum Bear replied "mmm … mmm"

Then even more to Amy's surprise, the other bear also made the same "mmm … mmm" sound.

Amy's eyes nearly popped out of her head she was so surprised. "There's more bears like you, Hum!" she gasped in amazement, whispering into Hum's ear.

"This is the Mum Bear," announced Mrs Estuary, waving her hand as she introduced the Mum Bear to Amy.

Suddenly, another little bear who was sitting next to the Mum Bear started to laugh and chuckle very loudly. It sounded so like a very happy baby's hearty laughter. The little bear just chuckled and chuckled away, putting a great big smile on Amy's face. This little bear was beautiful, with huge brown eyes and long eyelashes. It had long, luxurious, soft, sandy, goldie fur. The ends of the fur had been dip-dyed with pink tints. The little bear wore a bright pink skirt and matching pink bow on her head. This little bear's name was Bebe. She was a very happy little bear.

Then the Mum Bear made a very unexpected sound. "Shhh … shhh" she hushed, putting her paw to her mouth has she looked down at a cradle that was gentle rocking to and fro. There, laid in the cradle making small, sleepy, snorey sounds, was another adorable little bear. Like Bebe, this bear also had long, luxurious, soft, sandy, goldie fur. The ends of this bear's fur had been dip-dyed with pale blue tints. He wore a pair of pale blue shorts and had a pale blue ribbon tied in a bow around his neck. This bear's name was Schnuggle Budd. Amy could not take her eyes off these adorable little bears, they were just so cute.

"Aww, aww," she cooed as she just stood there staring and staring at them. They made her go all gaga and soppy.

The Mum Bear, Bebe and Schnuggle Budd made up the most wonderful family of gorgeous bears. Each one could do something different and had their own special style. Amy was holding the Hum Bear and she could feel his little heart gently beating in his chest. "Pe-pum, pe-pum" went the sound of the Hum Bear's heartbeat. Then the glow of his little golden heart shone through his little navy blue waistcoat. Hum was very happy indeed to see the other three bears.

Mrs Estuary suggested to Amy that perhaps she should sit her Hum Bear next to the Mum Bear while she looked at a book that she had found that would be suitable for Lillie. Amy sat

Hum down next to the Mum Bear. She was very interested in the book that Mrs Estuary had brought to show her. The title was *Grace and Glad.* Amy was pleased with this book and was sure that Lillie would like it, particularly because Lillie's middle name was Grace. Amy flicked through the first few pages. The story was about two sisters, whose names were Grace and Glad Darling. Grace had golden blonde curly hair and blue eyes. She was very "girlie" and loved her dolls' house and dollies. In contrast, Glad had straight, dark-brown hair but the same vivid blue eyes as her sister. Glad was more of a tomboy than her sister and preferred climbing trees and wearing denim dungarees. In the story, the two sisters helped another little girl with a magic mirror.

"Yes, this will be the perfect book for Lillie. Can you put it away for me until next week when I can come back and pay for It?" said Amy to Mrs Estuary.

"Sure. No problem," replied Mrs Estuary kindly. She took another look at Amy and said, "You look like an honest girl. You can take the book now and pay for it later. All our contact details, including our telephone number, are on the back of the book. You can ring us any time from Monday to Saturday before the shop closes at 6 o'clock."

"Thank you so much," said Amy, putting the book into her rucksack, tucking it in between her recorder and the gingerbread stars. She slotted her arms through the straps and pulled the rucksack firmly onto her back. "It's time I must be getting back to my family and friends, before they start missing me."

Then something else caught Amy's attention. She noticed a very, very old clock in a long oak case standing against the wall. It was the old antique clock she had heard striking the time earlier. The grandfather clock had a very large pendulum which swung to and fro. It made a loud tick-tock sound. The large circular face had the numbers 1 to 12 circled around its edge. It also had two hands, a large one and a small one. The small hand was pointing to the number 5 and the large hand was pointing to the number 2. The time was ten minutes past five. This gave Amy another reminder it was time she was getting back to her family and friends. The antique grandfather clock was quite tall, much bigger than Amy. At first, Amy hardly noticed two more bears standing at each side of the big, old antique clock.

One bear had grey fur and wore a smart, dark, pin-striped suit. He wore a gold pocket watch attached to his suit. He was standing straight and upright. The other bear had black fur. He wore white shorts and a waistcoat that had ragged frayed edges. He wore a white baseball cap on his head. He was leaning back against the side of the clock in a very carefree casual manner. This bear wore a very thick, chunky gold watch upon his wrist. These two bears were timekeeper bears who helped Mr Estuary to regulate time, when he was involved in any time-travel activities.

The two bears both stepped forward and bowed to Amy. She was absolutely amazed as the grey bear started to speak in rhyme.

Hello Amy.
Listen and see, you can count on me
I am the Num Bear, not a Dumb Bear,
I speak in rhyme, I beat in time.
Listen and see, you can count on me.
One, two, three, bend your knee,
Four, five, six, fingers clicks,
Seven, eight, nine, you are doing fine,
Number ten, start again.
Now Amy, repeat after me.
Very soon we will have a tune.
With half a chance, you can make a dance.
Listen and see, you can count on me.

Amy was amazed. She followed the Num Bear's instructions and soon she was having great fun, counting, clicking and dancing about.

If Amy was not utterly entranced by all this, what happened next was so truly astonishing that it made her stand perfectly still. The black bear started rapping! All Amy could do was just stand, stare and giggle in astonishment.

I am the Rapp Bear.
I'm a wear a cap bear,
I am friend of the Num Bear,
We are an unlikely pair.
He's my best mate,
We do not have no hate.
Listen to him,
He is not dim.
He is the Num Bear,
He's a do any sum bear.
We are the timekeepers
Not the over sleepers.
We don't make no fuss,
You can count on us.
We have learnt to time-travel,
Seen wonders to unravel.
Been to the North Pole and back,
Even seen in Santa's sack.
We have seen dinosaurs roam
Then returned safely home.

We have visited the future
And seen a City of Culture.
We have been through the ages,
Then landed back upon these pages.

The Rapp Bear stopped rapping. Amy was so taken by surprise she wasn't quite sure what to say or do. All she could do was ask the question,

"B ... b ... but how?" she asked nervously.

The Num Bear and the Rapp Bear replied together in rhyme.

Many things you won't know, until you grow,
Then you'll remember, some old bear,
When you was just a kid again,
Doing what you did again
The future will tell
If you learn your lesson well.

This was all quite a riddle for Amy. She had no idea what it could all mean. All she could do was reply in just one word, "WOW!"

To this the Num Bear and the Rapp Bear replied, "NOW, GO ASK HOWARD HOW!"

Both bears swung their arms and pointed across the room to the left. Amy turned around and walked in the direction that they were pointing . Something else caught her eye ... another teddy bear! This bear was a dark chocolate-brown colour and he was quite large and stout. He wore a black mortarboard cap on his head and a long black cape-like gown, similar to ones Amy had seen some of her teachers wearing. The bear's eyes were very large and googly and rolled about in his head. The bear's large googly eyes looked over a small pair of spectacles which were perched upon the end of his long, dark snout . He was holding a cane in his hand and was pointing to a blackboard. On the blackboard was a star drawn in chalk. Inside the star was written the word "HOW". Then she saw another chalk-drawn star with the word "MEG" written inside it. Amy almost fell back in surprise as she suddenly remembered the dream she had had the other week. This was when she was asking the question, "Who took the Hum Bear away from the spot where Granny Anne had placed him near the leafy green bush all those years ago?" Amy was becoming more and more bewildered as she remembered that, in her dream, she was in a room full of books with some clocks, teddies and drawings of horses, dogs and birds. Amy also recalled the Hum Bear showing her stars with the words MEG and HOW on them. Something very strange was happening. Very strange indeed, but yet it was all quite magical.

Amy scratched her head. She was feeling rather baffled, but at the same time felt rather excited.

"I don't understand what is happening. It is definitely the first time I have ever been to your shop, but I have visited it before in my dream," she told Mrs Estuary.

Mrs Estuary nodded and smiled at Amy telling her not to worry and that everything would be fine. "This bear's name is Howard. He is a teacher bear and knows just about everything. You just have to ask him "HOW?""

"HOW?" repeated Amy in surprise.

Howard's large googly eyes started to spin and roll about even more in his head. Then, in a deep booming voice that appeared to echo and bounce around the room, he said, "**Hello Amy. You don't need to ask me how. I already know what your question is.**"

Howard pointed to a book with a picture of a birthday cake with nine candles upon it.

Amy was speechless. Her jaw dropped and she just stood there with her mouth gaping wide open. She was so shocked at hearing Howard speak so clearly, and even more so that he already knew her question.

"Do you remember your birthday wish Amy, when you blew out the nine candles on your cake?" asked Howard.

"Yeees," replied Amy, drawing out her reply with hesitation.

"You haven't told anyone what you wished for, have you Amy?" said Howard sounding quite important.

"No, no, not a single soul," replied Amy truthfully.

"Amy," Howard went on to say in his deep booming voice, "You are a child of the future. We need to teach you well so that you may show others the right way."

"Wh..., wh..., what do you mean?" asked Amy nervously.

"Do you remember ever going to the Hull Fair*?" asked Howard.

"Oh yes!" said Amy, remembering with excitement all the thrills of the fair. "I loved all the rides, especially the helter-skelter and galloping horses. Best of all, I won a gold fish in a bowl on the "hook a duck". My mum bought me a brightly coloured windmill which I used to blow and blow and it would spin around and around and all the bright colours would mix up together." Amy chuckled as she recalled her memory with much fondness.

"In the future, Amy, there will be many giant-like windmills on both land and sea. They will

_____
* See page 196

be very, very tall and pale and will be known as wind turbines. There will also be a very deep giant aquarium near the River Humber where thousands of different fish will live. These are good things about the future. But beware Amy, not all is good for the children of the future. Children stay indoors too much, playing with their games and phones, not taking enough exercise, and eating too many sweets and chocolates. Some children are very unhealthy," said Howard, who was a very wise bear.

"Really?" came Amy's astonished reply, thinking of all the fun she and her friends had had recently, playing and running about outside. Amy also loved riding her bike. She loved the outdoors and could not imagine staying indoors too much.

The very idea of playing with a phone seemed extremely strange to Amy. She had no idea about mobile phones or social media. Back in the 1980s, no one had home computers. The only telephones she knew were landlines and the phones were very large with numbers on a circular dialling ring.

"What about these giant windmills or wind turbines. What are these things for?" asked Amy quizzically, curiosity getting the better of her.

"There are for energy," replied Howard.

"I don't understand what you mean. I know that if I eat up my dinners my food gives me energy. How do you get energy from a wind turbine?""It's a different sort of energy. It provides electricity for many things like lighting and keeping homes warm. Well, that's all you need to know about wind turbines for now, Amy. First you need to find out the answer to your birthday wish," said Howard. "Take this book with the picture of the birthday cake outside, blow on it and make your wish," instructed Howard.

Amy picked up the book with the picture of the birthday cake upon it and started to carry it outside. Then she heard a voice call out, "Finished". It was Art Robbie with his finished sketches of Ruby, Faithful, Craven and the leafy green bush.

"I've coloured them in and now I need to put the picture outside in the sun to let the paint dry," said Art Robbie, carefully carrying the picture and placing it on the ground outside. Amy placed the book with the picture of the birthday cake next to Art Robbie's paintings. She stood admiring the paintings. Art Robbie had got all the colours painted exactly right and they made all the animals look even more life-like. Craven was painted with his little red breast.

Ruby was painted with a glossy dark-brown coat and purple head collar. Faithful had been painted with all her black and white markings in the correct places. Even the shading on the leafy green bush made it appear to shimmer in the sunlight.

"Don't forget your Hum Bear," Mrs Estuary reminded Amy.

Amy walked quickly back inside the shop and picked up Hum from where he was sitting near the Mum Bear, and she brought him outside.

When Amy and Hum where back outside, Amy was very surprised to see that, as if by magic, the birthday cake picture had popped up out of the book and the nine candles were alight, flickering on the top of the cake.

"It's still your birthday Amy. You can make another wish or make the same wish you made earlier," called out Howard.

Amy had a burning desire to know who had taken the Hum Bear away from the spot where Granny Anne had placed him near the leafy green bush all those years ago. The same bear that Granny Anne called her Bertie Bear. So, of course, she was going to make her same wish … Oh, she so wanted her wish to come true. She was so excited she completely forgot about the time and returning back to her family and friends.

Amy held the Hum Bear close in her arms, crossing her fingers at the same time. She closed her eyes tightly, took a deep breath, made her wish and then blew and blew at the nine candles. She opened her eyes. The candles had blown out and the white smoke from them was blowing, swirling and circling over Art Robbie's painting. The hazy outlines of the drawings started to shimmer and shake. Amy could not believe what happened next. The drawings rose up very slowly, then sprang to life before her very eyes, as if new life had been breathed into them. First Ruby came to life, popping up out of the painting. She stood up on her four lanky legs, shook her mane and let out a long neigh. Then Faithful followed. She stood up on her short black-and-white legs, let out a woof and wagged her long black tail with a white tip. Craven puffed out his little red feathery breast. He spread out his little wings, gave a tweet and flew up into the air. Then the leafy green bush "grew up" out of the sketch, its leaves shaking as if they were being blown about in a wind. Ruby and Faithful stretched their legs and started to run about on the nearby grassy field. Craven hovered and swooped about in the air above Ruby and Faithful. The two animals and the little bird appeared to be having fun together.

The Hum Bear started to spin like a whirly bird, whipping Amy up into the air. Faster and faster. They were spinning like a tornado. Then whoosh! They landed on the grass near a small, green bush. Amy lay on the grass keeping tight hold of Hum. She was feeling a little dazed and dizzy. Ruby, Faithful and Craven were nowhere to be seen. Amy lay there quietly for a minute trying to get her breath back. As she lay there she heard voices singing. Amy recognised the song. It was the same song about scarlet ribbons she had sung at her birthday with her Granny Anne. She sat up, still feeling a bit dazed. Then she looked across the grass and saw a little girl singing with her father. A crowd gathered around and applauded them.

Amy then realised she had gone back in time by many, many years. To the time when her Granny Anne was a young girl, about the same age as Amy.

Amy sat quietly behind the green bush cuddling her Hum Bear. No one else could see them sitting there. She was wondering what she was going to do next when, suddenly, she heard a voice coming from the other side of the green bush.

"Gotcha! You're coming with me!" said a girl's voice, speaking sharply.

Amy drew in her breath again. At first, she thought the girl was speaking to her. But no, she was mistaken. The girl hadn't seen Amy. It was Meg, the girl who once tried to take Granny Anne's Bertie Bear off her. Meg didn't see Amy sitting behind the green bush. Neither did Amy notice that there was a teddy bear sitting on the other side of the bush. There, sitting in front of the green bush, was Bertie Bear on the spot where Granny Anne had placed him. Bertie Bear looked exactly the same as the Hum Bear but he was not wearing a little navy blue waistcoat like the Hum Bear did. Meg had her eye firmly fixed upon him. Roughly, she grabbed hold of Bertie Bear and ran off with him.

Amy was so angry. How dare this girl try to steal her Granny Anne's bear.

"C'mon Hum," said Amy bravely to the Hum Bear. "We are going to follow her and find out what she is up to."

TWO

Amy was running along holding Hum tightly, her rucksack with its contents bouncing along on her back. She kept looking straight in front of her, determined to find out what Meg was up to. She could see Meg in the distance turning a corner, and then she disappeared.

"What do we do now?" she whispered to Hum.

Then Amy heard voices calling to her, "Over here."Amy looked up and, to her amazement, saw two girls standing there beckoning to her. At first she thought she recognised them but couldn't quite think where she might have seen them before. Amy stood and scratched her head, as she studied their faces and the clothes they wore. One girl had golden blonde curls; the other had straight, dark-brown hair. They both had the same vivid blue eyes. One girl wore a pink dress, the other a pair of denim dungarees.

"No, it can't be!" exclaimed Amy.

Both girls just smiled and nodded as if they had read Amy's mind.

"Are you Grace and Glad Darling?" asked Amy, hardly able to believe her own eyes.

"Yes, that's right," replied Glad.

"But ... but ... you ... you can't be," said Amy, hardly able to get her words out. "But you are not real, you are from the story book that I got for my friend Lillie."

The sisters looked at each other and smiled. "There's no time to explain," said Glad.

"Yes, that's another story," added Grace. "You must be very quick now. No time to lose."

"Here's something to help you," said Glad, handing Amy an oval-shaped silver-rimmed hand mirror.

"Is this a magic mirror like the one in the story book called *Grace and Glad* which is about you two helping someone with a magic mirror?" asked Amy, all excited and surprised at the same time.

"Yes, that's right, "said Grace and Glad together.

"Oh this is so weird and crazy. I have never known anything so strange in my life. I have bought a book for my friend Lillie and then I meet the main characters. AND THEN I seem to appear as part of the story," said Amy in disbelief.

"Yep, awesome!" said Glad.

"Magic!" said Grace.

The girls continued to tell Amy that if she held the mirror up in front of her, did a twirl and turned the mirror around so that the back of it was facing her, she would become completely invisible. This would help her glide along quickly and unseen. They told her not to allow anyone else to use it and, when she did not need it, to put it into her rucksack. They gave Amy the directions of how to get to Meg's house. "Next street on the left into Beaming Way, all the way down, then turn right and go past a bombed building site into Garden Avenue. Then down by a long row of houses, turn left again and you'll be nearly there. Meg lives at number four Rainmore Road." Amy took the mirror in her right hand while keeping tight hold of Hum in her left arm. Her rucksack was placed firmly on her back. She held up the mirror and looked in it. Her reflection stared back at her. Her face looked frightened. Amy did feel quite scared.

"Fortune favours the brave. Don't be afraid Amy," said Glad, firmly giving encouragement.

"Yes and you've got the Hum Bear right by your side. You'll be fine," Grace said reassuringly.

Amy took another look in the mirror; she looked herself right in the eyes, tilted her chin up, cocked her head back and gave herself a big smile. A braver, more confident- looking Amy stared back at her. She did a twirl, turned the mirror around and immediately she became invisible."Great, the magic mirror is working perfectly," said Grace to Glad.

"We can't see you at all. Amy are you still there?" called out Glad.

"Oh yes," Amy called back in an excited voice. "This is great fun. I am about 60 cm up in the air and feel as light as a feather. I think Hum is enjoying it as well." Hum's familiar "mmm … mmm" could be heard.

Grace and Glad called out to Amy, "We'll meet you back at the green bush later and you can tell us all your news. Hope you find out what you need to know. When you return to us later, we may not able to see you if the mirror's magic is still working. You will need to untwirl twice and spin the magic mirror back around three times until you are facing it. By then you should be able to see your own reflection. Don't be too long, you have to be back at the Estuary Bookshop before closing time at six o'clock. This is really important Amy, because if you are any later, you will never be able to get back in and you will be lost in time for ever."

Amy wasn't paying proper attention to this important information Grace and Glad had told her. She was too distracted and having too much fun floating about in the air invisibly.

"See you later," called back Amy, only half listening to what Grace and Glad had to say. "Wheeee!"

THREE

A my was soon on her way again. The time and place was Hull in the 1940s, not long after the end of the Second World War. Off she went, quickly gliding along down Beaming Way, unseen on the sunny side of the street. There were no cars about, just a young delivery boy riding a big bicycle with a huge basket on the front, delivering food parcels. There was also a coalman and a milkman making their deliveries using horse-drawn carts. Some children were playing with their skipping ropes. Two young girls were playing hopscotch for which they had drawn the grid on the road with a piece of chalk. Amy thought to herself how dangerous it would be for her to play in the road with her friends because there was much more traffic about in her time. These children could play in the street and did not have to worry about all the dangers from cars.

The girls finished their game of hopscotch and paused. They sat down on the kerb edge and were happily chattering away to each other. Earlier, it had been raining heavily but the sun had dried up most of the rain. The girls never noticed that there was a large muddy puddle not far from where they were sitting. Neither did they notice an older boy on a bike lurking just around the corner. He was watching the girls and sniggering to himself. He was getting ready to stir up mischief. Suddenly, he started to ride his bike as fast as he could. He rode it right through the big muddy puddle, causing it to throw up a cold, wet spray of dirty water. The cold, wet, dirty water covered the girls. They were drenched! Their hair was sodden and flattened down onto their heads. Their face and clothes were speckled in dirty, muddy brown spots. They jumped to their feet, shivering and dripping with water. A lady came running down the street to help them. It was one of the young girls' mothers, who took them home to clean up.

Nobody knew that Amy had seen everything while she was hidden from sight behind the magic mirror. It made her feel very angry about what the nasty boy had done to the girls. "That boy really needs to be taught a lesson," she thought to herself. But there was no time to do anything. Amy had to be on her way and go and find Meg.

Amy turned a corner into Garden Avenue. She saw a row of about five or six terraced houses. The end house on the row had collapsed into a great pile of bricks. The houses were next to a field where there was a huge crater that had been left when a bomb had been dropped during the war. A lone figure of a man, dressed in a sailor's uniform, was standing there. He had served in the Royal Navy during the war and returned home to find his house had gone. It had been bombed away. All that remained was an enormous pile of bricks where his home had once been. Amy was so shocked at this sight that she halted in her tracks and almost dropped the magic mirror.

She took a deep breath and continued, invisibly gliding past the row of houses in Garden Avenue and then turning left again. She was in Rainmore Road. She looked down the street. There were many rows of old shabby houses with cracked windows. Then Amy caught sight of something out of the corner of her eye, running down the street and going through a broken gate to a house with a number 4 upon it. It was Meg, carrying Bertie Bear.

Silently and unseen, Amy caught up with Meg and followed her as she went in through the front door. The door slammed shut behind Amy with a loud bang, which startled her. The house felt cold and smelt of damp. The walls looked bleak and grey except for an old antique clock with a swinging pendulum. Amy paused as she passed by the clock. She thought that she recognised it but couldn't think where from. She shuddered. It wasn't a very nice place to live.

Then a man's voice shouted out from the back room, "IS THAT YOU, MEG?" It was Meg's stepfather.

"Yes father," replied Meg in a small voice.

"WELL YOU ARE LATE! YOU CAN GO TO YOUR ROOM WITHOUT ANY TEA!" The stepfather shouted back at her.

"Yes father," said Meg, again in the same small voice.

Amy felt very uneasy about the way Meg was spoken to by her stepfather. She also felt uneasy about the cold, bleak, uninviting home she had just entered secretly. It was so different from the feel of her own home which was always warm, bright and welcoming, with the smells of good home-cooked meals. Her mum was always pleased to see her return home from school and was interested to know what she had been doing.

Amy followed Meg up the creaking staircase, across the bare floorboards on the landing and into Meg's tiny bedroom. The small, dark, dull room contained nothing else but a small bed and a dressing table with a large mirror on it. There was no sign of any toys, books or pictures. Amy went and stood silently, unseen, next to the dressing table. She thought about her own bright, pink, warm bedroom that was so different from this room. Even her Wendy house at Somewhere Place had more toys than this empty drab bedroom.

Amy was starting to feel more and more uneasy about hiding in someone else's house. She had to remind herself that she was not going to do anything bad; that this girl had stolen her Granny Anne's Bertie Bear and something needed to be done about it. Amy was not too sure what she was going to do next.

Meg had no idea that Amy could see her. She started to speak to poor little Bertie Bear in such a way that it made Amy cringe. Meg grabbed hold of Bertie so roughly she nearly knocked all the stuffing out of him. Then she started to prod him hard in the chest with a thin bony finger.

"I KNOW you are no ordinary little bear. I've seen and heard how you helped that Anne Baker to sing. Even if it is a stupid song about scarlet ribbons. Her dad was so proud of her and everybody thinks she is wonderful. NOW YOU help me to sing like that and then people will like me too," shouted Meg at poor Bertie, prodding and bullying him. Amy was stunned.

Meg was suddenly interrupted when a loud, booming voice roared up the stairs. "WHO ARE YOU TALKING TO MEG? AND WHERE IS YOUR MOTHER? SHE HAS BEEN GONE ALL AFTERNOON!" It was Meg's stepfather shouting at her again.

Meg started to quake and tremble as she replied in a small voice, "I was just talking to myself father, and I don't know where mother is."

"Well if you have nothing better to do than talk to yourself you had better get down here, you lazy, good-for-nothing girl, and make yourself useful. The pots and kitchen floor need washing."

"Yes father," said Meg as she threw Bertie on the bed and ran down the stairs obediently to do her chores.

Now was Amy's chance. With Meg out of the room, she could just pick Bertie Bear up off the bed, hide him behind the magic mirror and take him back to the green bush. Amy was about to step forward when she felt the Hum Bear tugging her back.

"What is it Hum? Do you think we should just leave Bertie Bear lying there on the bed?"

"Mmm … mmm," replied the Hum Bear.

Amy wasn't at all sure what to do. This was a dreadful situation. She wanted to rescue Bertie so that he didn't have to suffer Meg's bullying. But yet, Meg was only an eleven-year-old-girl who had nothing and was being neglected and mistreated by her stepfather. This girl was desperate to be loved and cared for. Amy felt quite angry with Meg for how she was treating poor little Bertie but yet she couldn't but help feel sorry for her because she was living such an awful sad life.

"What are we going to do Hum? I never expected to find this happening," whispered Amy.

Hum didn't get a chance to make a murmur. Meg had finished her chores and was walking back into the bedroom. She was hungry and not feeling very happy. She walked over to the bed and roughly snatched hold of Bertie.

"NOW THEN, WHERE WERE WE?" she snarled at poor Bertie. She was scowling, causing her eyebrows to meet in the middle. She started prodding and bullying Bertie again. Meg believed that Bertie Bear could help her to be a good singer. Again and again she prodded him in the chest, bossing him about and demanding that he help make her into a good singer. Poor Bertie was helpless. He couldn't do anything.

Amy stood there watching, unseen by Meg. She was beginning to regret that she hadn't taken Bertie Bear away earlier when she had the chance. Meg snarled and prodded at Bertie once more. Amy could hardly bear it any longer and let out a huge gasp. Meg heard Amy's gasp. She swung around with her ears pricked up. Still wearing the scowl on her face and her finger pointed into Bertie's chest, she walked over to the dressing table.

"Who's there?" she said in a puzzled voice. She looked up, searching for where the gasp had come from. She then caught sight of her own scowling reflection in the dressing table mirror.

Then the magic mirror started to work its magic. Unseen by Meg, it had the power to "freeze" Meg's face. It did so and she was unable to change her scowling expression. Neither could she pull her finger away from Bertie's chest. The other mirror on the dressing table was reflecting Meg's scowling face back to her. She could do nothing but take a good look at herself in her mirror. She did not like what she could see and felt afraid of her own reflection. She tried to alter her face but it would not change. It was stuck. She tried and tried to pull and tug her thin bony finger away from Bertie's chest but it simply would not budge.

Taking another good hard look at herself, Meg had a sudden change of heart. The magic mirror was showing Meg that what she was doing was wrong. She was shocked to see her nasty looking scowling face with her eyebrows meeting in the middle of her forehead. Bertie looked terrified. Meg started to feel quite ashamed of how she was treating him. Then a huge tear welled up in her eye and trickled down her cheek, melting, softening and wiping away the harsh expression upon her face. The tear fell on to the end of Meg's finger and she was able to pull it away from Bertie's chest. The tear fell off her finger with a splash, onto Bertie's chest and soaked deep, right into his fur. Then something wonderful happened. A heartbeat could be heard "pe-pum, pe-pum" and a golden glow shone out from Bertie's chest in rhythm with the heartbeat. The little golden heartbeat had happened in the same way as when Amy's tear had landed on the Hum Bear's chest at the "Big, old house" when she was in foster care. Meg spoke to Bertie Bear telling him how sorry she was for being so nasty to him and that she would never treat him so badly ever again. She smiled at Bertie, giving him a big squeeze and a hug.

Just then, Meg spotted something lying on the floor. It was a scarlet red ribbon. Amy hadn't noticed that it had fallen out of her hair and was lying on the floor. Meg picked up the brightly coloured ribbon wondering where on earth it had come from. There were some very strange things happening. Meg took the ribbon and tied it into a bow in her own hair. Meg's flame-red hair and the red ribbon offered a chink of bright colour in the grim and cheerless room. Meg stared at herself in the dressing table mirror and managed another little smile. She didn't usually have much to smile about.

Then, suddenly, something else happened, Something similar to what had happened to Amy once before when she was with Bridget Bear in her bedroom at her mum's house., A long ray of sunshine, which appeared to have a long pointed gold finger on the end of it streamed in through Meg's bedroom window. The lightstream gently stroked Meg's face. The whole room was bathed in sunlight, making it much warmer and brighter. Meg's green eyes sparkled and her smile grew larger and larger until she had a broad grin right across her face. Then the lightstream disappeared through the window.

Meg skipped happily over to her bed and pulled out a box from underneath it. From it she took out a pair of ballet shoes and put them on. Putting her arms up above her head and standing on her tiptoes, Meg did a pirouette. Carefully watching herself in the mirror, she began to hum a tune to herself, then began to dance. Meg danced and danced and leapt and pirouetted around the room, watching herself in the mirror. She danced until she could dance no more and then just flopped happily down onto her bed. She pulled off her ballet shoes and hid them away in the box under her bed. She picked up Bertie Bear and gave him a big cuddle. Meg said to Bertie, "I'm going to stop thinking about being a singer. I probably can't sing anyway. I'm going to practice my dancing from now on."

Suddenly, loud voices and a lot of shouting could be heard from downstairs. Meg felt frightened and pulled Bertie Bear closer to her. Meg's mother had returned home and she had some people with her. Her stepfather sounded very angry and stormed out of the house, shouting out, "I'M NEVER COMING BACK HERE!" The door slammed shut after him. Meg breathed a sigh of relief. She was really pleased to hear this.

Everything went quiet, then Meg's mother walked into the bedroom with another little red-haired girl. It was Meg's little sister, Emma.

"We don't have to be afraid of that Stan Beastly any more. He's gone and good riddance!

He is not your real father. Your real father was a war hero. He was a soldier who went away to fight in the war and never came back. I have been speaking to some very kind people. They have told us that a soldier's wife and children should not have to live in fear and they are going to help us. Meg, I need you to help look after your little sister while I make some plans. Things are going to be very different from now on."

"Oh yes, mother, of course I will help look after Emma," replied Meg, really happy to hear her mother's news.

Mother left Emma with Meg in her bedroom. They both played nicely together with Bertie Bear. Then Meg started to brush Emma's hair. She put it in a ponytail and took the red ribbon out of her own hair and tied it in a bow in Emma's hair. They both sat together, smiling into the mirror. These two girls hardly had anything at all. It had only taken something very simple like a teddy bear and a red ribbon to put a smile on their faces.

All this time Amy had been watching, silent and unseen. She was amazed at what had happened. What was even more amazing was the remarkable likeness of Meg and Emma to Amy's friends, the twins Megan and Gemma who had the same flame-red hair. When Amy had gone back in time forty years, could it be possible that she had found the twins' grandmother and aunt when they were both children? It was incredible.

Amy decided that she had seen enough and she was going to leave Bertie Bear with Meg. He was the only toy these two children had. They would be facing difficult times and Bertie Bear could help them through these. It was time for Amy to go and get back to her own time in the 1980s. But before she left the house, she remembered that Meg was hungry, so she left behind some of the baked gingerbread stars for the girls to eat. Meg had no idea where the gingerbread stars came from but she didn't care, she was so hungry. She shared them with her little sister Emma and they both thoroughly enjoyed them.

Still clutching tight hold of Hum and the magic mirror, Amy left Meg's home feeling much better than she did when she had first arrived. She glided swiftly along up Rainmore Road turned the corner into Garden Avenue, past the row of houses and back down Beaming Way. Amy floated along daydreaming, lost deep in thought. She had always thought that Granny Anne's Bertie Bear and her Hum Bear were the same bear. Now she was not so sure. They looked the same, identical in fact, but somehow different. It was just a feeling Amy had that she was not too sure about. Maybe they were two separate bears that just looked the same? Maybe when she got back to the Estuary Bookshop she would ask Howard more questions.

Suddenly, as she was gliding swiftly and silently unseen along Beaming Way, she spotted the same nasty boy with the bicycle, who she had seen earlier. He was there, lurking around the corner sniggering to himself, ready to make mischief on those two poor girls again. The two girls were playing with their skipping ropes and skipping closer and closer to the hopscotch that they had chalked up earlier. They hadn't seen another big dirty puddle.

The nasty boy had seen it. He was watching the girls skipping closer and closer to it. The nasty boy got on his bike and started racing towards them, ready to play the same mean trick on them again. But Amy had other ideas. He was not going to get away with this again. The magic mirror started to do more magic. The sun was shining brightly in the sky. Suddenly, the mirror reflected the bright sun into the eyes of the two girls. It dazzled them so much, it made them stop and jump back out of the way of the approaching boy.

Then the magic mirror turned its attention on the big muddy puddle. It used its power to make the puddle bigger, muddier and deeper.

Amy also had her part to play. The mirror and Amy were completely unseen by anyone else. Suddenly, Amy lifted the mirror up slightly and stretched her feet down to the ground. All that was visible was a pair of feet wearing a pair of shoes and socks. Amy couldn't resist the hopscotch. She plunged one foot into the number one square, then two feet into the second and third squares, and so on. She hopped and jumped along the hopscotch until she reached square number 10. Then she pulled her feet back up behind the magic mirror. Amy was hidden from sight again.

The nasty boy on his bike couldn't believe his eyes at the sight of a pair of feet without a body playing hopscotch. He wasn't looking at what he was doing and fell off his bike. He landed with a great big SPLASH! right in the big muddy puddle. He was drenched. Soaked wet through right up to his neck. His face and hair were splattered with mud. He picked up his bike, which was bent and buckled, and pushed it as he made his way back home.

All that the two girls had seen was the nasty boy fall into the big muddy puddle.

"Serves you right," the two girls called out to him. "That will teach you a lesson!"

The boy didn't say anything. He just skulked off on his way. He wouldn't be bothering the girls again.Amy smiled to herself and was off again. "C'mon Hum, we need to be getting back to the Estuary Bookshop. There are still more questions I need answering," she said to the Hum Bear who she was still holding tightly.

"Mmm … mmm" replied the Hum Bear.

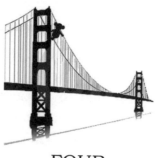

FOUR

Amy continued gliding along unseen, lost in her daydreams until, eventually, she was back at the green bush. Then she saw Grace and Glad but, to her horror, something strange had happened to the girls. They were both frozen still like statues. The pair of them both looked as though they had been running, with their arms and legs poised like the snapshot of a runner that had been frozen in action.

"OH, WHAT HAS HAPPENED?" called out Amy in horror.

What Amy didn't realise was that strange things could happen when you are involved in time travel. Things that are not easy to understand. Grace and Glad had become stuck somewhere in a time trap.

Amy was trying to remember the instructions they had given her about how they were able to see her again. She had to think very carefully, then she remembered. Untwirl twice and spin the magic mirror around three times. Amy did this and, hey presto! she was no longer invisible. There she stood with her feet firmly on the ground, looking all around, wondering what she was going to do about Grace and Glad. Everything appeared silent and still. Even the green bush appeared to be "frozen". There were no sounds of people or birds singing, just the empty sound of silence.

Amy held Hum even tighter. She was feeling afraid again. She wanted to get back to her own time at the Estuary Bookshop, but she knew she just could not leave Grace and Glad as they were. What was she to do? Then she had an idea that maybe there could be a clue in the storybook of *Grace and Glad* that she had got for Lillie. She reached inside her rucksack and pulled out the book. She took a quick peep inside and she saw a picture of a hand holding the magic mirror and moving it over and above and circling it around the girls. Amy took the mirror and copied the action she had seen in the story book. After a few minutes of swirling the mirror about like a scanner above and around the girls, they started to move and became like themselves once more.

"Phew!" said Amy with relief.

"Hello Amy," said Glad as if she had no idea she had just come out of a frozen trance. "Did you find out what happened to your Granny Anne's teddy bear?" asked Grace, no longer stuck like a mannequin.

"Bertie Bear is going to be just fine. Thank you for letting me use your magic mirror, it has been a great help. But now I must be getting back to my own time. My mother will be very worried if I have been gone too long," said Amy, relieved to hear Grace and Glad's voices again.

"The magic mirror will help you again to get you back to your own time," Grace told her. But before Grace could say any more, a strange, distant wailing, droning sound could be heard. The magic mirror started to flash a red flashing light. The glass became steamed and misty. Some warning words appeared on the mirror's steamed-up glass. Loudly and in unison, the three girls all read out the first word: "MENACES!" And then the next words "DANGER! DANGER!" All of a sudden, the distant droning sound was becoming nearer and nearer and louder and louder. There was a dark, dotted, pattern of movement in the sky which swooped and darted about. It wasn't a flock of birds. But what could it be? Amy was bewildered and clutched the Hum Bear tightly. Grace and Glad knew what it was. They quickly explained to Amy that this was a swarm of evil, wild, stinging hornets. These wild hornets are the enemies of the honey bee. They want to destroy the honey bees. Without the honey bees to pollinate plants and flowers, we would no longer have any fruit and flowers and much damage would be done to all our natural surroundings. It was really very serious.

As the wild hornets drew nearer, their noise was turning into a deafening, high-pitched buzz. And the swarm was heading in the direction of Hum and the girls.

"Oh, do you think they are going to attack us?" shrieked Amy in alarm, clutching the Hum Bear even tighter.

"Well, I don't think they will attack you, Amy, but they could try and attack us," said Glad, looking at Grace with a worried look upon her face.

"Well, why should they attack you two and not me?" asked Amy with a mixture of curiosity and fright.

"It is because they know you are not from our time and they want to follow you through a time trap to get to the future and destroy many thousands of honey bees," said Grace.

"Oh no. What shall we do? I can't leave you here to be attacked, neither can I return to my own time and risk letting the wild hornets following me through a time trap," said Amy, becoming more and more afraid. "Perhaps we could hide behind the leafy green bush and the hornets will not see us."

The three girls and the Hum Bear crouched down behind the leafy green bush, hushed up quietly hoping not to be seen. But it was no use. The wild hornets knew that they were hiding. The huge swarm gathered directly above the leafy green bush, ready to launch an attack on the girls. Then, suddenly, the Hum Bear forced himself out of Amy's arms and propelled himself upwards, spinning right into the middle of the swarm of angry hornets. Hum spun round and round so fast that the swarm was whipped up like a tornado, killing off many of the evil hornets. The rest of the hornets flew off in different directions.

"Oh Hum, you are so brave. You protected us like a super hero," said Amy, taking the Hum Bear back into her arms and giving him a cuddle. She turned to Grace and Glad. "Do you think they have gone?" asked Amy in a low voice.

"Maybe," whispered back Glad, not feeling too sure.

"We'll just have to wait quietly for a while and see what happens," added Grace.

But as they all waited quietly, the distant droning and buzzing of the hornets started to draw nearer and nearer again.

Once again, the Hum Bear forced himself out of Amy's arms, propelling himself up into the air to protect the girls. The swarm of evil hornets was even angrier and wanted revenge on the Hum Bear.

Suddenly Glad had an idea. She picked up the magic mirror and pointed it upwards to where the Hum Bear was hovering. The Hum Bear's image could be seen in the mirror.

"MAGNIFY," shouted Glad, ordering the mirror to work its magic.

Immediately, the Hum Bear grew to be three metres tall. He spun around and around in the air looking like a giant goliath of a bear. He was now much stronger and more powerful. The hornets swarmed nearer and nearer and were about to fire their stinging darts at the Hum Bear. But the gigantic Hum Bear hummed and spun so fast he deflected away all the hornets and killed them all. Hum fought on as long as he was able, but he was injured by some of the stinging darts that were stuck in his fur. He waivered about in the air like a giant flat balloon and was beginning to fall down.

Then, suddenly, two more smaller swarms of hornets were coming from opposite directions to attack the Hum Bear.

"Just try and stay up in the air a little longer," called out Grace. "I have an idea."

Hum was very tired and injured but, bravely, he stayed wavering in the air to try and fight off the hornets and defend the girls.

The two opposite swarms of hornets made two separate circles, gathering speed and becoming noisier and noisier. They were as fast as two speeding trains. Each angry swarm raged towards the Hum Bear to launch another attack.

Just as the army of charging hornets was about to attack the Hum Bear, Glad pointed the magic mirror at him.

"MINIMISE!" Glad shouted, ordering the mirror to do its magic once again.

Immediately, the Hum Bear shrunk to the size of 2 cm and fell down into the green bush. The two charging swarms of hornets fired their stinging darts, missed the Hum Bear and instead attacked and completely killed each other. Not one evil hornet was left.

The magic mirror was no longer flashing red and the word "SAFETY" appeared on the glass.

"But what about Hum? Is he all right?" asked Amy, looking around for her teddy bear.

"Don't worry, here he is. Good as new," said Glad as she waved the magic mirror over the green bush and called out the word "RESTORE". The mirror worked its magic once more and Grace pulled the Hum Bear out of the green bush and gave him back to Amy. Amy was very pleased to have Hum back and to find he was no longer suffering any injuries from the hornets' attack.

"We really can't waste any more time now, we have to get you back to your own time," said the girls.

"We will swirl the mirror over you and you must do another twirl. Then the rest will be up to the help of your whirling Hum Bear."

"There's another thing you need to know that is very important," Glad warned Amy. "When you return to 1984, at the time that you re-enter the Estuary Bookshop, you must walk in backwards until you are right inside. Be very careful not to blow out your birthday cake candles again. You must also get back before the bookshop closes when the clock strikes 6 o'clock or else time no longer flies by. Time will just drag by so slowly that everything will seem like ages and ages and everything will be so boring."

"No time to explain any more. You must hurry now Amy. Are you ready?" asked Grace.

"Ready," replied Amy nervously as she took her place near the green bush.

Grace and Glad took turns to give the magic mirror a good swirl over and above Amy's head and down and around her arms. Amy did a little twirl. Then the Hum Bear started to whirl and whirl and she took off from the ground like a helicopter. Amy closed her eyes tightly and clutched the Hum Bear close to her chest. She started to spin faster and faster until she was whipped up like a tornado. Then, with a great whoosh, she came to a halt and landed with her feet firmly on the ground.

Amy felt a little dazed and dizzy and she just stood still with her eyes closed for a few minutes. Then she opened them and looked all around. She had no idea where she was. She was in a place she had never been before. She rubbed her eyes, hardly believing what she could see. Where was the leafy green bush? Where was the Estuary Bookshop?

At first Amy thought she must be dreaming for there, before her very eyes, she could see some dinosaurs! Where on earth was she?

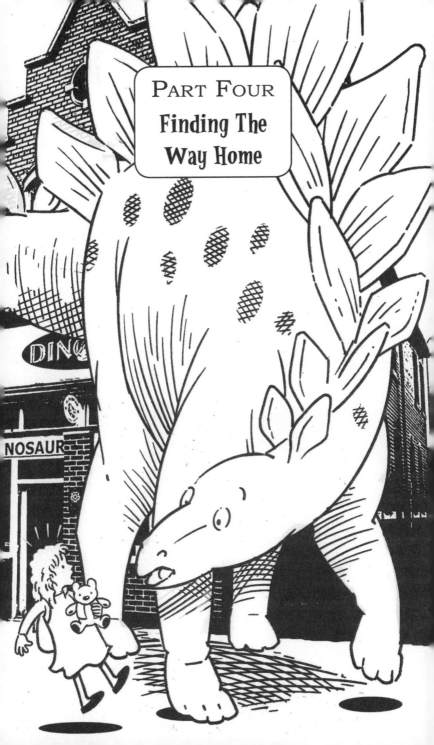

PART FOUR

Finding The Way Home

ONE

A my stood staring into the face of a dinosaur which was there, right in front of her. The dinosaur was stooped over. He had a huge face. This very large face was staring right back into Amy's small face. The dinosaur's long jagged neck sloped up from behind its head looking like a flight of stairs, curving over onto the dinosaur's back. It was a stegosaurus! At first, Amy was very worried that she had gone far, far back in time to when dinosaurs roamed the earth. Fortunately, it was not a real dinosaur. Amy had not gone back in time but she had overshot 1984 and had landed near the city centre of Hull. She was looking into the window of a museum called "The Dinostar Experience*". When Amy realised that she wasn't in some prehistoric age she was very

---

* See page 195

relieved. But she was also very worried about where she actually was.

Amy looked up and saw a street sign on an old brick wall that read HUMBER STREET. She started to figure out that perhaps this street was near the River Humber or the Humber Bridge. She stood there, looking all around and down Humber Street. There were a lot of old buildings. Some of the buildings were painted in bright colours with pictures of fish, crabs and a seal on the walls. She also noticed a group of older children walking by holding very small, thin boxes. One boy had the little box held near his ear. Some girls were looking down at the little boxes held in their hands. One girl appeared to be moving her finger as if she was stroking the small, thin box. Another boy was tapping his finger on his box. It looked rather like a chicken pecking at seeds. They were all concentrating very hard on these small, slim boxes. Amy thought this was very strange. What she did not know was that many children now owned a mobile phone. Amy had never seen or heard of a mobile phone before. The only type of telephone she had ever seen or used was a landline one.

While Amy was standing there wondering what she was going to do next, she noticed a car pull up and park not far from where she was standing. A woman stepped out of the car together with a rather plump-looking girl eating chocolate.

"I hope we won't be walking very far. I hate walking. I like being at home watching my DVDs and playing my games," announced the girl, stuffing another chocolate into her mouth.

"You can't stay indoors all the time, sweetheart, watching DVDs and playing games. These things can be good but too much is bad for you. I loved playing outdoors when I was a girl," said her mother.

"WELL! This is 2014 and it's different from when you were a girl!" replied the daughter, speaking very rudely to her mother. "Anyway I WANT my tablet," demanded the girl in a very spoilt manner.

The mother and daughter carried on walking.

Amy stood there looking, listening and almost reeling with shock. 2014! Was this for real? Had she really travelled across time and was now in the year 2014? Amy was also very puzzled about the girl demanding a tablet. The only tablet she had ever heard of was a sort of pill that people took if they were ill or in pain. She did not know it was some type of modern technology. There was no such thing as this type of tablet in Amy's own time of 1984.

Amy suddenly remembered what Howard, the teacher bear, had told her about the children of the future. That children would become very unhealthy, eating too much chocolate and spending too much time indoors, playing with their games and phones. It appeared that Howard was right and he really did know many, many things.

"What are we going to do now?" Amy whispered to the Hum Bear.

The Hum Bear pointed with his paw. Clutching Hum tightly in her arms, Amy walked in the direction he was pointing. She crossed over another road and walked quickly a bit further along. Soon she was walking on a brick-paved area where there was a statue of a man. Behind the statue, Amy could see a river. It was the River Humber. Amy was so pleased to see the river. She was also fascinated and surprised by the many sorts of people visiting the area. White people, black people, coffee-coloured people, Chinese people and women in long clothing and headscarves. Amy also heard them talking in different languages.

Some people were walking about. Amy saw a bald-headed man with his black-haired wife and their two young children. The bald-headed man spoke to his children.

"Look over here, Anthony. Look over here, Anna-Sofia. There is The Deep*," said the children's father as he pointed to a dramatic shaped building made from glass.

"Daddy, are we going to see the fish at The Deep?" said the little boy.

"Yes," the man replied. "There are penguins, too. We will wait here to meet your cousins Lenni and Zeb. They are really looking forward to visiting The Deep with you."

A fair-haired couple with two blonde curly-haired little boys ran up to meet their cousins. All the young children ran happily to meet each other. They were all very excited about going to see the fish and penguins at The Deep.

Amy stood and watched the two families as they made their way towards The Deep. She looked up and across towards an enormous building. It almost resembled a boat that pointed up towards the sky with blue glass at the prow end. Amy stood and stared, she had never seen anything quite like it before in her life.

So this must be what Howard had meant when he had spoke of a deep aquarium where thousands of different fish would live, thought Amy to herself in amazement. More and more of what Howard had told her was coming true.

_____
* See page 194

Amy scanned her eyes over the river until she was looking in the opposite direction from The Deep. She became curious about a blurred shape that she could see in the distance, further down the river. She scurried along over more of the brick-paved area until she was walking on a wooden pier. She looked down and noticed some fish shapes carved in the wooden boards. This was part of Hull's Fish Trail*.

Amy walked over the wooden boards of the pier. She held her hand up over her eyes, shielding them from the bright sunlight. Screwing up her eyes, she was almost squinting in the sunlight. She peered along over the river. She could still see the blurred shape in the distance, far beyond the craggy edges of the bending, wriggling, riverbank that was lined with tall buildings. The blurred shape was something that Amy recognised. She kept staring at it until it came more and more into focus. The hazy mist over the river was lifting. 'Yes!' Amy thought to herself. There, far in the distance, she could just make out a familiar sight – it was the Humber Bridge. There it stood in the distance, as strong and solid and proud as ever. It looked quite small from where Amy was standing. But there was no mistaking the bridge's twin towers, still looming

---

* See page 195 & 198

loftily, rising high up from the riverbank. It was a real sight for sore eyes.

"It's the Humber Bridge," she whispered excitedly into Hum's ear. "It looks a long, long way away, but perhaps if we can find our way to it maybe we can find our way to the Estuary Bookshop and find our way back home. I do so miss my family and friends, but I am so glad that I still have you, Hum. Amy gave the Hum Bear a big squeeze.

Hum was also happy to see the Humber Bridge again. He murmured "mmm ... mmm" in his usual way and then his little heart started to beat with its "pe-pum, pe-pum" sound. His golden heartbeat shone, flashing on and off and shining through his little navy blue waistcoat.

Amy carried on walking. She passed the Minerva pub and turned a corner. She saw lots and lots of boats and yachts bobbing about on the water. It was the Hull Marina*, a harbour for many, many pleasure boats. "Oooh, Grandad Charlie would love this place," she thought to herself, remembering her grandfather's love of boats.

Amy walked on a little further gaining a spring in her step. The Hum Bear was joggling about in her arms and her rucksack was bouncing

---

* See page 195

about on her back. Suddenly, she spotted a dark-skinned man sitting alone on a bench near a large black cannon. He looked as though he was lost in thought as he sat there dreamily. He started to tap away gently on a pair of bongo drums. He was not aware of the little girl walking towards him. Then Amy halted, stopped still in her tracks in surprise. She wasn't too sure but she really felt as though she recognised the man and was somehow drawn towards him. Then came another surprise. The Hum Bear suddenly started to hum a tune into Amy's ear. This put a huge smile on Amy's face as she recalled what it was. She promptly delved into her rucksack and pulled out her recorder and began playing the tune. Playing her recorder, she started to walk nearer and nearer to the man. He was sitting with his back to her and didn't see her approaching. His ears pricked up. He recognised the tune and started to beat his drums to the rhythm of the tune Amy was playing. He started to play louder and louder and Amy tooted away on her recorder as she walked towards him until she stood next to him. The man spun around. They both stopped playing their instruments and stared.

"AMY!" exclaimed the man.

"WILBER!" exclaimed Amy at the same time. She wasn't sure whether to laugh or cry. They had been brought together by the music, the very same piece of music they used to play together back in the garden at Somewhere Place and also at Amy's birthday party ...!

Both of them stood looking at each other in bewilderment, hardly able to believe their own eyes. The boy Wilber that Amy had once known was now a grown man, working in the Hull City Centre. He was an electrician and was making preparations for the Freedom Festival*, a big yearly event that was about to be staged in the city.

Wilber told Amy that people were very excited and looking forward to Hull being the UK City of Culture in 2017*.

"Oh wow!" said Amy. "I can see that Hull has already changed and come a long way. I can hardly wait to see what is in store in 2017." Amy suddenly remembered part of the Rapp Bear's words about the future and seeing a City of Culture.

Amy liked this bright new world she had discovered but, even so, she was missing her own time very, very much.

"But now, how on earth are you still only a nine-year-old girl?" asked Wilber, very puzzled indeed.

---

* See page 194

"It's a very long story, Wilber, " replied Amy. She went on to tell him all about her time-travel adventures. How she had gone back in time to the 1940s and how she had tried to get to 1984 but had landed in 2014. And that she really did need to get back to her own time in 1984.

"Wow! That's incredible, Amy," said Wilber. "I know. I will contact KC. He'll know what to do. I'm sure he will be able to help you get back to 1984."

"KC? Where is he? Is he OK? Are his legs better now?" Amy questioned Wilber excitedly. She almost forgot for a moment that she was in a different time zone.

"KC is fine. He hasn't worn his calipers for many years. He will be at work over there in the town centre," said Wilber, pointing in the direction beyond the Marina. "I will send him a text to tell him to look out for you."

"A text? What is a text?" asked Amy, looking bewildered. She had never heard of texting before.

Wilber showed her what texting was on his mobile phone. Amy then realised that the teenagers she had seen earlier tapping the little flat boxes had been using their mobile phones.

"That's fantastic. What a great way to keep in touch with people. Modern technology is marvellous. I hope I will have a mobile phone one day. I want the world to know what a great place Hull is," said Amy, as if she could hardly wait for the day to arrive when she would own a mobile phone of her very own.

"And what about your twin sisters, Megan and Gemma? Are they all right?" asked Amy.

"Oh yes, they are fine. You would hardly know that they were twins now, they look so different and each prefers a quite different style. But they both still love dancing and performing. Megan is a dance teacher and Gemma is a drama teacher," said Wilber, with a broad grin on his face. Gone was the surly looking boy that Amy once knew. Wilber had grown into a very happy, confident, cheerful man.

Just then, one of Wilber's workmates called out to him with a sense of urgency. "Wilber, quick, over here. There's a problem with the electrical equipment and we need an electrician to fix it or else the Freedom Festival will be ruined."

"I have to go and hurry now, Amy. I am needed to correct an electrical fault. Don't worry. I have sent a text to KC and he will come and find you. Just keep heading in that direction," said Wilber, pointing with his finger. "Pass by all the white yachts in the Marina until you see a larger black boat with the word SPURN written on it in large white letters. You should also see a pelican crossing nearby where you can cross the road safely. When you have crossed the road, turn left and look out for signs for the big new police station. KC will probably be driving about around there."

Wilber and Amy said their goodbyes and waved to each other. Wilber went off to do his electrician's job. Amy ran off in the direction that Wilber had sent her.

Amy jogged along over an old cobbled area and then onto a newer paved area that was near the side of the Marina. The shiny, bright-white boats and yachts gleamed as they bobbed gently on the water in the harbour. The water glistened as the sunlight danced over the tiny rippling waves that licked the sides of the moored boats. Many birds were flying about too.

Amy observed and listened carefully to all the new sights and sounds she had found. It was a lovely place to visit for all people, young or old. She was thinking how much her family and friends would love to see this lovely area. She looked in amazement to see a land train go by on a sightseeing tour. All the passengers appeared to be enjoying themselves and the train driver was making them laugh. Amy was also wondering about KC and if he ever made it to be a bus driver, which had been his boyhood dream.

Before she knew it, Amy had almost got to the black ship with the word SPURN written upon it. She saw the pelican crossing that Wilber had told her about. Some other people were also crossing the road, so she crossed safely with them. On the other side of the busy road, Amy forgot which way Wilber told her to go and, instead of turning left, she turned the wrong way and turned to her right.

She wandered along near a busy road, then she whispered to Hum, "I think we have come the wrong way, maybe we could try this street?" She took a left turn into a small, quiet, narrow street and then wandered along some more quiet narrow streets. She felt hopelessly lost.

Suddenly, Amy almost stumbled over something. It was a pair of legs wearing a pair of scruffy old trainers, belonging to a man slumped in a doorway. As Amy stumbled, she almost fell over so she stopped to gain her balance. The man in the doorway tried to stand up. He held a can in his hand and was slurping a drink from it. He stood up, but wobbled so much he almost lost his balance. This gave Amy quite a fright. She did not like the look of this tall, thin, smelly man who was wearing a dirty, tatty, grey, hooded jacket.

He had a very pale face and hollow cheeks. He had red-rimmed eyes that sank into his pale, drawn face. When he spoke, he slurred his words and the liquid he had drunk from his can dribbled down his stubbly unshaven chin. When he opened his mouth to speak, he showed a set of very decayed, uneven, broken, brown teeth.

"What have we here, little girl?" slurred the man pointing his bony finger with dirty nibbled nails at the Hum Bear.

"This ... this is my friend," replied Amy, stuttering her words out nervously. She was feeling very scared and she pulled the Hum Bear closer to her.

"I'll be your friend," said the man, still slurring his words and forcing a false smile which displayed his rotten teeth, making them look even worse.

"No!" replied Amy very sharply. "My mum told me not to speak to strangers!"

The horrible hooded man told Amy that he knew her mum and that he would take Amy to her, but he was telling big lies. Amy didn't believe he knew her mum. She had to think very fast. She did not want this horrible man to take her away. Suddenly, the Hum Bear started to tap her rucksack. Amy remembered she still had some gingerbread stars in there. So she delved into her bag and pulled one out.

The man was very hungry and stared at the gingerbread star.

"Give it to me!" he demanded, his mouth watering as he feasted his eyes upon the tasty looking gingerbread star.

"Here, catch," shouted Amy as she hurled the gingerbread star as high into the sky as it could possibly go, to try and distract the horrible hooded man.

The horrible hooded man turned to look up to where she had thrown the gingerbread star. Amy ran off in the other direction as fast as she could. She ran and ran as fast as her little legs would carry her. Faster and faster she ran through the narrow cobbled streets and alleys. She passed under an archway and through an open market place and by the big old Holy Trinity church. Amy ran down the side of the church, then noticed another little side street. She thought that perhaps if she ran down this small narrow street, she might be able to lose the horrible hooded man and give him the slip. She raced down the short, narrow, cobbled street. When she reached the end, she turned the corner and found she was near the long busy road again. She glanced back and there was no sign of the horrible hooded man. She was puffing and panting and so out of breath she really had to stop and get her breath back.

Amy stood still and took another quick look behind her. No sign of the horrible hooded man. She breathed a sigh of relief. Then, as she glanced to her left, she saw some huge bright green posters with pictures of giant white windmills on them. At first Amy didn't know what they were until she read a large sign. Then she realised that they were the giant wind turbines, like the ones that Howard had described to her. The ones that help to produce energy. Amy was amazed. Something else that Howard had told her was also true.

Suddenly, Amy was startled by the sound of heavy footsteps thudding behind her. She felt sure that it must be the horrible hooded man still trying to catch her. She was so afraid she did not dare spare one moment to turn around and look at him. Off she sped once more, fleeing around a large sweeping corner and into another street. She was still very tired from all the running and knew she could hardly run anymore. Then Amy saw a very big statue of a golden man sitting upon a golden horse. It was the King Billy Statue*.

Still Amy did not dare to stop to take a better look, neither did she dare to look back to see if the horrible hooded man was still chasing her.

---

* See page 195

Oh how she wished that the statue of the man on the golden horse could be Lauren's horse, Ruby, and that she could just climb up onto Ruby's back and gallop away. Oh, she so wanted to gallop far, far away and escape from the horrible hooded man whose footsteps she thought she could hear drumming in her ears.

She ran on a little further. Then, not far from the statue, she saw a golden telephone box. Then Amy had an idea. She knew she could not run much further so she decided to try and hide in the golden telephone box.

Amy's heart was pounding and pounding in her chest and she was gasping for breath. She was just about to open the door of the golden telephone box when a man's hand grabbed her shoulder. With the last bit of breath Amy could muster up, she screamed and shrieked out, "LET ME GO! LET ME GO!" But the hand had grabbed hold of her very, very firmly.

Amy froze with fear and took a sideward glance. Out of the corner of her eye she saw a large hand gripping her shoulder. Then she noticed a very long arm, then a very bright, yellow waistcoat. It wasn't the horrible hooded man. This hand holding her shoulder belonged to the "long arm of the law". Amy turned and looked again. She was so relieved to see that it was not the horrible hooded man but a policeman. Then she could also see a policewoman further down the street, arresting the horrible hooded man. Amy let out a huge sigh of relief. "Phew …"

The police had seen everything that had happened. It had all been captured on CCTV. (closed-circuit television cameras).

The policewoman snapped a pair of handcuffs on the wrists of the horrible hooded man. Then she called out to the policeman, "I will deal with this man if you can deal with the little girl," before marching the horrible hooded man away to the police station.

The policeman let go of Amy's shoulder and looked at her.

"Amy?" he exclaimed, sounding a little puzzled.

"How do you know my name?" asked Amy, in an equally puzzled voice.

The policeman grinned and held up the gingerbread star that still had Amy's name written upon it in white icing sugar. But now the gingerbread star also had some silver glitter dust upon it too. The policeman had caught it when it fell back down after Amy had hurled it up very high into the sky. He handed the gingerbread star back to Amy and she popped it into the Hum Bear's pocket.

Then the policeman surprised Amy by telling her that he had received a text from Wilber.

Amy stared at him. There was no mistaking that cheeky grin. It was the face of her young friend KC, who was now grown up to be a man.

"KC! Is that really you?" asked Amy, almost in disbelief.

"Yes it is," the policeman replied. "I am PC KC and very proud to serve the local community."

"I thought you wanted to be a bus driver when you grew up?" said Amy, recalling their conversation back at Somewhere Place.

KC chuckled and grinned again. "Oh, I used to drive a bus, but now that I am in the police force, I also drive a police car. The police are working very hard in the streets of Hull to keep it a safe place. You do not have to worry any more about that man in the hoodie that was chasing you. He will be locked up and dealt with by the Law."Amy was very relieved to hear this.

Amy noticed that KC was very tall and no longer wore calipers on his legs and she asked him if his legs were better.

"My legs are much stronger and better now and I haven't needed to wear my calipers for many years," replied KC.

"What about your twin sisters, Megan and Gemma? I do miss my friends. Are they all right?" asked Amy, curiosity getting the better of her.

Another broad grin spread over KC's face as he spoke about his sisters. "You wouldn't recognise them now, they don't even look like twins any more. Gemma has short, red, spikey hair, dangly earrings and bright-coloured clothes. She teaches dance.

Megan also looks totally different. She has very black hair and wears a lot of black clothes and has her nose pierced with a silver stud. Megan teaches drama. They may look very different but they work very well together teaching children performing arts. They are planning a big song and dance extravaganza for Hull City of Culture in 2017."

"Oh wow, that sounds really exciting," said Amy, really happy to hear this news about her friends. But she simply could not imagine Megan and Gemma without their long ginger ponytails.

Amy looked at the gold-painted telephone box. She could remember seeing many public telephone boxes back in 1984 but they were all painted a cream colour. Amy also remembered going with her mum to a public telephone box and making a telephone call to her friend because they didn't have a landline telephone at their house.

KC told Amy that this was a special telephone box which had been painted gold to honour a young man from Hull named Luke Campbell, who had won an Olympic gold medal for boxing in the 2012 Olympic Games.

"Oh, that's fantastic!" said Amy.

"But now we are going to have to find a way of getting you back to your own time, Amy," said KC, speaking a little more seriously.

"Somehow I need to get in touch with Mr Estuary from the Estuary Bookshop," replied Amy.

"I don't think that there is an Estuary Bookshop now. I've never heard of it," said KC, looking rather puzzled.

"What are we going to do?" asked Amy in despair.

Both Amy and KC stood and thought about it for a moment, pondering as to what to do next. Then Amy felt the Hum Bear tapping her rucksack with his paw. Amy reached inside and pulled out the book, *Grace and Glad.* The book was turned back to front and there, on the back, Amy saw the sticker that Mrs Estuary had put there giving the contact details of the Estuary Bookshop. Immediately Amy knew what to do. She would use the telephone in the golden telephone box and call Mr Estuary at his bookshop.

She picked up the large handset and put it to her ear. She was pleased to hear a dialling tone so she rang the telephone number. At first, she could just hear a repeating beeping sound and no one answered the phone.

Looking worried, she turned to KC and asked what else she could do.

"Try again," KC urged her. "It may be engaged or it could just be a bad line making it difficult to get through."

Amy tried ringing the number again and then she was very, very relieved to hear a familiar voice. It was Mr Estuary. "Hello Amy," he said, "I've been waiting to hear from you."

"Oh, Mr Estuary, I am so happy to hear your voice," said Amy in delight as she spoke into the big handset. "Can you help me get back to my own time please. I am missing my family and friends so much."

"Don't worry Amy, we will have you back soon, but first I need to know your exact location."

"Well, I know that I am somewhere near the town centre of Hull and I am in a gold telephone box and there is a picture inside of Luke Campbell who won a gold medal at the Olympic Games," Amy told him.

"Very good Amy, I know exactly where you are so I can use my special time equipment in my office. I will have you back in no time. Just go and wait outside the telephone box. This won't take very long," Mr Estuary reassured her.

Amy stepped outside the telephone box and told KC that soon Mr Estuary was going to transport her back to 1984. Then she said goodbye to KC.

"Goodbye, Amy. Take care of yourself," said KC, stepping back and waving his hand.

Amy stood excitedly outside the telephone box. She could hardly wait to see her family and friends again. With her eyes closed tight and her fingers crossed, she held the Hum Bear tightly in her arms. She looked down at Hum who was holding the gingerbread star with Amy's name iced upon it. Amy smiled at Hum and gave him a gentle squeeze. "Mmm ... mmm" went the Hum Bear and his little golden heartbeat went "pe-pum, pe-pum".Still keeping her eyes tightly closed, with her fingers crossed and holding her breath, Amy stood waiting eagerly. Then she waited some more and still nothing happened. Amy hardly dared to look, so she just opened one eye. KC had gone and the sky was becoming darker. Suddenly the sky started to look brighter. Amy opened both her eyes wide and then she had to close them quickly again as a very bright light dazzled her. It was the Lightstream, the long ray of light with the long golden finger. The long golden finger pointed at Amy, then, as quick as a flash, the Lightstream whizzed down out of the sky and wrapped itself around her. It spun Amy and swirled her around and around until she disappeared from view from outside the golden telephone box.

A strong wind started to blow and the distant sails of the wind turbines started to spin around and around. Very swiftly, Amy spun and spun. She was hurling through space and time, still clutching the Hum Bear.

Then Amy landed heavily with a bump. In a blink of an eye she was back in 1984. "Ouch," yelped Amy, as she landed rather heavily back at the leafy green bush. But as she landed, she could not keep hold of the Hum Bear. He was jolted so hard that she let go and he flew out of Amy's arms. He cartwheeled, topsy-turvy, through the air until he tumbled down and came to rest at the other side of the leafy green bush.

Amy was a little dazed and sat up, rubbing her sore back. Then she saw and heard something that made her shiver and made her whole body shake. A girl's voice said "ouch". Amy peered through the leaves of the leafy green bush and saw a young girl rubbing her grazed knees. The young girl scooped up the Hum Bear, put him over her shoulder and covered him over with her long goldie-brown hair. Then the young girl ran off to catch up with a group of children further up the road.

Amy stood up, staring in disbelief and confusion. She was now back to 1984 but she was in a time lap and had returned a few months too early. She had arrived at the leafy green bush at the time when her former self had first found the Hum Bear. Amy just did not know what to do. Already she was feeling completely lost without her precious Hum Bear snuggled up in her arms. She had been on a very long journey with Hum and she felt too tired to make any sense of what was happening. Feeling lost and forlorn she started to weep.

Meanwhile, back at the Estuary Bookshop, Mr Estuary was in his office frantically pressing buttons and switches. He called to Mrs Estuary. "Something has gone terribly wrong on the Time Travel Continuum. Amy has arrived at the leafy green bush a bit too early and she has almost bumped into her former self. While I make some adjustments and try to bend time, please can you just check outside and see what is happening with Art Robbie's painting and the birthday cake candles."

Mrs Estuary could hear the urgency in her husband's voice and immediately ran outside to where Amy had made her birthday wish. To her horror, she could see that the candle flames had just gone out and they were beginning to melt. There was a lot of black smoke coming from the candles. On the picture that Art Robbie had painted of the green leafy bush, the leaves where starting to crinkle, wither and turn brown. There was no sign of the painted figures of Ruby, Faithful and Craven.

"Oh! No! No! What has happened? Where can Amy be?" cried out Mrs Estuary, flinging up her arms and putting her hands on her head in despair.

She ran back inside the bookshop to report what she had seen to Mr Estuary. Mrs Estuary was very worried what had happened to Amy.

"Don't worry, Eileen, I think I have corrected the problem," called out Mr Estuary, trying to reassure his worried wife. "All in good time we should have Amy back here before the grandfather clock strikes 6 o'clock," he called out as he worked frantically in his office, where he held his finger on a button. Then the Num Bear started counting numbers in seconds, minutes and hours very quickly. The Rapp Bear was rapping frantically. The timekeeper bears were assisting Mr Estuary in regulating time. The pendulum on the antique grandfather clock was swinging furiously. The hands on the old clock face where spinning round and round.

"Quickly Eileen, go and check the painting again," urged Mr Estuary.

Mrs Estuary ran back outside and looked again at the painting. She saw that the leaves on the leafy bush were returning to their green colour and the birthday cake candles started to have small flickering flames and the black smoke had disappeared. However, there was still no sign of Ruby, Faithful and Craven.

Meanwhile, something very mysterious was happening to Amy. She was standing there feeling very lonely without her Hum Bear. She looked up and stared at the Humber Bridge. All of a sudden, her legs started to run very, very quickly, out of her own control. But she wasn't moving anywhere, she just started to run faster and faster, her bent arms rapidly swinging back and forth at her sides. Amy was running and running on the same spot but not going anywhere. Before her very eyes, she could see sail boats moving faster than speed boats, passing swiftly along the River Humber. Then the sky above the Humber Bridge turned dark. Suddenly, she could see a flaming bright sunrise burst out from the dark sky. In the bright light of the morning sky, birds flew past at an incredible speed. The sky turned pale blue with many little fluffy white clouds dashing across the sky. These clouds quickly grew larger and larger and darker and darker until they burst with heavy rainfall. Then the sun shone again and an arc of a beautiful coloured rainbow appeared then disappeared. Then, as quickly as the sun had risen, it went down and there was a magnificent red sky as it set and disappeared into the dark night sky. The moon and the stars appeared, shining brightly and twinkling like diamonds in the night sky over the tall, strong, dark, towers of the Humber Bridge. Everything was moving at a very, very rapid speed. Morning, noon and night were flashing past repeatedly before her very eyes. It was like watching a DVD with the fast forward button pressed. Amy paused and thought back to when Grandad Charlie told her that a red sky at night was a good sign. She also thought about what her mum had told her about her dad and that, while he was far away, he would give her the moon and the stars if he could.

Then everything started to slow down. Amy's little legs stopped running on the spot and slowly, slowly ground to a halt. She could hear bees buzzing and a butterfly fluttered by. Then she saw something floating along, gently, softly and slowly, up in the pale blue sky. There, twizzling and swirling in the light warm breeze, was a pink balloon with a long red ribbon attached to it. Suddenly, she heard a noise. It was a horse's neigh and a dog's bark. Then she heard a bird tweeting. Amy turned around and saw the hazy paint-streaked figures of Ruby and Faithful running towards her. Hovering above them and flying through the air she saw Craven. She started to cry tears of joy which rolled down her cheeks at the sight of her four-legged and feathered friends. She threw her arms around Faithful as she jumped up and licked all the tears away from her face. She patted and stroked both the animals before climbing up onto Ruby's back. Craven swooped down and rested upon Amy's shoulder. Gently, she gave him a little stroke and ruffled his feathers with her finger. Craven puffed out his little red breast proudly.

Amy whispered into Ruby's ear, "Oh Ruby, you must help me find my way back to the Estuary Bookshop. Please run and run as fast as you can. I must be back before the pendulum clock strikes 6 o'clock and the shop closes."

Ruby lifted up one of her front hooves, nodded her head and, with another neigh and a whinny, off she went, galloping as fast as she could. Faithful ran quickly behind them. There was not a lot of time left and Ruby ran like the wind. Amy had to hold on very tightly. Soon she could see the Estuary Bookshop. When she was almost there, Amy spotted the pink balloon again. The long red ribbon was wriggling and writhing about in the breeze just above the Estuary Bookshop. Craven jumped off Amy's shoulder and flew up into the air. He swooped over to where the pink balloon was hovering. He pecked hold of the red ribbon which was dangling in mid-air, hanging from the balloon. With the red ribbon held firmly in his beak, Craven flew back and brought the balloon to Amy. Amy smiled. Surely this must be the same pink balloon with the long dangly red ribbon that her mum had brought for her as a welcome home gift? The very same one that had carried the Hum Bear and taken him to Granny Anne? Somehow, the balloon had got caught up in the time lap and found its way back to Amy. She dismounted from Ruby and took hold of the long red ribbon. The balloon danced and bobbed about in the light warm breeze, just above Amy's head.

Amy walked over to the spot where Art Robbie had left his painting outside to dry. Ruby, Faithful and Craven followed her. Amy stood on the very spot where she had blown out the birthday cake candles and made her wish to find out what had happened to Granny Anne's Bertie Bear.

She closed her eyes tightly and wished and wished with all her heart to be back to the right time and see all her family and friends again. Suddenly, she started to spin and whirl. Faster and faster she twirled. The pink balloon also spun and whirled quickly. The red ribbon twizzled and twirled as well. Then they was a very LOUD BANG ... followed by silence. Amy thought that the balloon must have burst. But no, the pink balloon was nowhere to be seen. It had simply vanished into thin air. Ruby, Faithful and Craven had also disappeared.

Amy looked down and saw Art Robbie's wet painting of Ruby, Faithful, Craven and the leafy green bush. It was still the same as she remembered it to be; freshly painted and left out to dry in the warm sunshine. Nearby was the birthday cake with its nine candles flickering brightly. Amy knew she was back to the time before she blew out the cake candles and had made her wish.

She was so happy to be back she breathed out a long sigh of relief. "Phewwww" she sighed, letting out a long breath which, to her horror, nearly blew out the cake candles. Amy remembered Grace and Glad had warned her not to blow them out again. She gasped and drew the large breath of air back into her mouth. To her amazement, the cake candles started to slowly dim and melt until they no longer flickered. Just a very faint trace of grey smoke was all that could be seen. Everything appeared to be quiet and calm. Amy also recalled that Grace and Glad had told her she had to walk backwards into the Estuary Bookshop until she was right inside and she had to arrive back before the shop closed at 6 o'clock.

Following Grace and Glad's instructions, Amy started to walk backwards until she was inside the bookshop. All was silent except for the ticking of the old pendulum clock on the wall. Then the silence was broken as the clock struck 6 o'clock. Amy breathed another sigh of relief. She had made it back in time and was back inside the bookshop before it closed at 6 o'clock.

Suddenly, Amy heard a quiet whispering sound going "shhh, shhh," followed first by a little chuckling sound, then a sleepy, snorey sound, followed by a "mmm ... mmm". Amy started to half turn around and, out of the corner of her eye, saw the Mum Bear, Bebe and Schnuggle Bud. It was the family of gorgeous bears in the very same place they had been before Amy had gone travelling through time.

Then Amy heard a woman's voice. It was Mrs Estuary. She could hardly believe her ears. Mrs Estuary was speaking.

"Don't forget your Hum Bear," Mrs Estuary reminded Amy.

Amy took a few more steps backwards and turned around. To her great surprise and excitement ... there ... sitting next to the Mum Bear, she saw her precious Hum Bear. Amy was back to the very point in time when she had picked up the Hum Bear! Everything was now at the correct moment before she had left the Estuary Bookshop.

The Hum Bear looked at Amy with his big brown eyes and with the half smile on the side of his face. He started to murmur his familiar "mmm ... mmm" sounds. Then the sound of his little golden heartbeat could be heard, "pe-pum, pe- pum" and his little golden heart could be seen glowing through his little navy blue waistcoat.

Amy scooped up the Hum Bear and gave him the biggest squeeze ever.

"I've got you back! I've got you back!" she squealed delightedly, almost jumping for joy.

Just then, Mr Estuary walked out of his office. "All done for the day. Time to close up the bookshop," he said.

Amy looked up at the pendulum clock on the wall that had just struck 6 o'clock. She was puzzled. She recognised the pendulum clock but could not recall where she had seen it before. Then she remembered. It was the same as the one she had seen standing in the hall in Meg's house in Rainmore Road.

Mrs Estuary walked over and stood beside Amy, very pleased to see that she had returned safely.

"Hello Amy, are you all right?" asked Mrs Estuary.

"Well, I'm a bit puzzled," replied Amy. "I thought that Granny Anne's Bertie Bear and my Hum Bear were the same bear, but now I am not so sure. And what about this antique pendulum clock standing near Mr Estuary's office that has just struck 6 o'clock? I'm sure it is the same one I saw at Meg's house in Rainmore Road."

"Come with me Amy. I have something to tell you. I think you are ready to hear what I have to say," said Mrs Estuary, putting an arm around Amy and guiding her along to another room.

Mrs Estuary opened a door and gently ushered Amy into a small room which she called her sewing room. Amy looked all around and saw a sewing machine and lots of fur fabrics. There were also lots of shelves with boxes of pins, needles, bobbins of cotton, and brightly coloured ribbons and pieces of cloth.

"This is the room where I make the teddy bears," Mrs Estuary told Amy.

"Did you make the Mum Bear, Bebe, Schnuggle Bud, the Num Bear, the Rapp Bear and Howard?" asked Amy curiously.

"Yes, I made all the bears, with the help of Mr Estuary. He made the programs for the bears to make them into the individual special little bears that they are.""That's wonderful," replied Amy. "Did you make Bridget, Bart and Bo-Jo Bear as well"?

"Yes, we made Bridget, Bart and Bo-Jo too. I took Bart and Bo-Jo to KC when he was ill in hospital."

"Bart and Bo-Jo really helped KC. It was really difficult for him when he had to wear calipers on his legs. He really enjoyed playing with the teddy bears. In fact all of us, Wilber, Megan, Gemma and everyone else, even the grown-ups, enjoyed seeing us all having so much fun," said Amy, smiling fondly as she remembered them all together singing, dancing and playing with the bears and the musical instruments.

Mrs Estuary was very pleased to hear all about this. She really wanted children to be helped by the bears and for children to love and enjoy the special little bears that she and Mr Estuary had made, especially children who were in need, like Amy and her friends who were in foster care.

Amy had more questions to ask Mrs Estuary about the Hum Bear and Bertie Bear. Amy had believed that the Hum Bear and Bertie Bear had been the same bear. Now she was unclear about these bears. She was in for another surprising shock.

"Come and sit down over here, Amy," said Mrs Estuary softly. "I have something to show you."

Mrs Estuary pulled out a very old, flat box. Inside the box there were two parcels wrapped up in old newspaper. Mrs Estuary unwrapped the first smaller parcel and inside was a pair of old ballet shoes. Amy stared at them looking very puzzled. Then Mrs Estuary pointed to the date on the newspaper. It was 1954. She pointed to a headline written in the newspaper. HULL BALLERINA MARRIES HULL SEAMAN. It was about a young lady named Meg, who was a talented ballerina and had married a local fisherman named Jim Johnson. Amy was becoming more and more baffled, but all was about to be revealed. Mrs Estuary unwrapped the second parcel inside which was a very tired-looking old teddy bear, complete with a yellow patch on his arm, stitched in black cotton.

Amy's eyes grew wider and wider as she just stared at the teddy bear in amazement. She could not believe it. Surely this had to be Bertie, the very same teddy bear that Meg had stolen from Granny Anne all those years ago. The very same teddy bear that Amy had left with Meg in her room at Rainmore Road.

"But I don't understand how all this is happening," said Amy, feeling very, very baffled.

Mrs Estuary looked down and smiled at Amy and started to explain everything to her.

"Before Mr Estuary and I had our bookshop, we also owned a second-hand and used goods shop. People would bring unwanted goods to us, we would buy them and then sell them at a profit. One day, just over nine years ago, a young man named Jamie came to the shop. He was helping his old uncle Jim clear out his attic from a really nice house in Beaming Way. Among the items was an old pendulum clock and this old wooden box containing the ballet shoes and this old teddy bear, that had once belonged to his old Aunt Meg.

Jamie really liked the old teddy bear. He told me that his wife was going to have a baby and that, when he returned home from his next fishing trip, he wanted to get a new teddy bear just like this one for their new baby. I told Jamie that I could make a brand new teddy bear, the exact copy of the old one. He was delighted and said that he would collect it on his return. Sadly, Jamie never returned as he was lost at sea. You thought that Bertie Bear and the Hum Bear were the same bear, but they are actually two separate bears that look exactly the same."

"So, was this man who brought Bertie Bear to your shop my dad?" asked Amy, burning with curiosity.

"Well, that does appears to be so," Mrs Estuary told her. "What is your full name, Amy?"

"My full name is Amy Johnson*," replied Amy.

"Well, this young man's full name was Jamie Johnson, so I am certain he must have been your father. Which also means that you are the one that he wanted the new teddy bear for. Somehow the Hum Bear really found his way to you," said Mrs Estuary, with a tear in her eye.

Amy looked at the Hum Bear, smiled and gave him a big hug. "You have always been a very special bear, Hum," she told him softly. "Now you are even more special than I ever could imagine. I

_____
* See page 197

will never, ever part with you. I am also glad that I gave you the name Hum, especially so because my dad will have sailed out on a trawler from the port of Hull on the River Humber."

Amy hugged and thanked Mrs Estuary for making the Hum Bear. It was now time for her to get back to her family and friends at the Humber Bridge where she had left them clearing up after her birthday party. She took one last look around the bookshop and she and Hum both waved goodbye to the Mum Bear, Bebe and Schnuggle Budd. The Mum Bear smiled, waved and winked her eye. Bebe chuckled, giggled and laughed. Schnuggle Budd opened his eyes and gave a little wriggle has he lay in his cot. He then closed his eyes and went back to sleep, making his gentle little sleepy snorey sounds.

Then Amy heard Howard, the Teacher Bear, speak in his deep strong voice. "AMY, WHATEVER YOU HAVE SEEN IN THE PAST OR FUTURE WHEN YOU HAVE BEEN TIME TRAVELLING, YOU MUST NOT TELL ANYONE. REMEMBER, AMY, YOU ARE A CHILD OF THE FUTURE. LEARN WELL AND SHOW THE WAY."

"I don't understand what you mean Howard," replied Amy in a puzzled voice.

"THERE ARE MANY THINGS YOU ARE TOO YOUNG TO UNDERSTAND, BUT ONE DAY YOU

WILL UNDERSTAND. WHATEVER YOU HAVE LEARNT FROM YOUR EXPERIENCES IN TIME TRAVEL, USE IT WELL," said Howard, speaking wisely.

"I have learnt a very valuable lesson and that is how important family and friends are. I have seen and met many different people on my travels, all very different, but yet we are all the same in many ways, and we all need one another," declared Amy in a voice that was very old and wise for a nine-year-old girl.

"WELL DONE, AMY. YOU HAVE LEARNT YOUR LESSON WELL. ALSO REMEMBER THAT YOUR VOICE IS A GIFT. USE IT WELL. PEOPLE WILL ENJOY YOUR SINGING," Howard told her.

"Oh, I hope so. I do like to sing," replied Amy happily.

Just then, the Hum Bear started to hum a tune into Amy's ear. It was the tune that had been one of Granny Anne's and Grandad Charlie's favourite about a *"place somewhere"*. It also served Amy as another reminder that it was time for her to be getting back to her family and friends.

"It's time for me to go now Howard. Thank you for everything," said Amy.

Howard said goodbye to Amy. Then all fell silent in the Estuary Bookshop. Amy took one last look around. Howard, the Mum Bear, Bebe and Schnuggle Budd stayed quietly in their own places, not making a sound. No one but Amy and Mr and Mrs Estuary would know what special qualities all these little bears had. They just looked like ordinary little toy teddy bears, waiting on the shelves for a child to come along and make them their very own.

Amy left the bookshop feeling happy and excited about seeing her family and friends once again. She walked off with a spring in her step and the Hum Bear humming the tune about Somewhere Place. Amy broke into song, happily singing along as the Hum Bear hummed.

Suddenly, she heard a voice calling out, "Amy". Then she heard a neigh and a clip-clop of horse's hooves, followed by a woof and a tweet. She looked up in the direction of the sounds. She saw Lauren riding Ruby. Then Faithful came bounding over as fast as she could to reach Amy. She jumped up at her and licked her face. She nearly knocked her over she was so excited to see her. It was the real Ruby and Faithful, not those that, magically, had come to life out of Art Robbie's painting.

"Amy, where have you been?" called out Lauren. "You have been gone for one full hour, Everyone is looking for you. You had better jump up here quickly onto Ruby's back. We can ride back to the others. It won't take long."

Amy and Hum climbed onto Ruby's back and they galloped away. Amy could hear the sounds of people's voices shouting out her name as everyone had joined in the search for her.

Very soon, Amy was back at the leafy green bush. She noticed something which surprised her. There, tied to the leafy green bush, was a big pink balloon with a long red ribbon attached to it. Amy climbed down off Ruby's back. Faithful was barking very loudly as if to let everyone know that Amy had been found. Amy's mum came running over to her and almost swept her off her feet as she gave her a great big hug. Everyone else came running over and was delighted to see Amy back safe and sound.

For Amy, it felt as though she hadn't seen everyone for months. She was so happy to see them all again. To everyone else, Amy had been missing for an hour and it had given them all quite a scare.

Amy's mum was very relieved to see her but quite cross with her for going off on her own without telling anyone where she was going.

"We were so worried about you that we have had to call the police," said Amy's mum.

"Oh, I'm really, really sorry for wandering away without letting you know. I will never do it again. I promise I will always ask you if I am allowed to go anywhere," said Amy truthfully.

Suddenly, Billy, one of the boys from the "big old house", shouted out, "Look, there's a "jam sandwich"!""What are you talking about?" asked Granny Anne, looking very puzzled. "Every bit of the food has been eaten up, there's nothing left."

"No, I don't mean a real jam sandwich that you eat," laughed Billy. "A 'jam sandwich' is the name local kids call police cars." Billy pointed as a long white car with a red stripe across the middle drove up. Granny Anne smiled. Now she could see plainly why the car was given that nickname.

A tall policeman stepped out of the white police car. He went over to speak with Amy's mum. She let him know that Amy had been found, safe and well. The policeman was pleased to hear this and that Amy hadn't come to any harm. He gave all the children a good talk on the dangers of wandering off and that they should never to talk to strangers.

KC really liked the policeman who showed him his car and let him try on his policeman's helmet. KC loved it."I want to be a policeman and drive a police car when I grow up," said

KC, with his small face beaming under the large police helmet.

"I think you could be a very good policeman one day KC, if you try hard," Amy told him.

Amy turned to the Hum Bear and smiled. The Hum Bear smiled back. "Mmm … mmm" he murmured in his usual way and gave Amy a cheeky wink. For they both knew KC would be a very good policeman one day.

The next day Amy and her mum was visiting her grandparents at Somewhere Place. Amy's mum sent her out to play in the garden with Wilber, Megan Gemma and KC. Her mum had received a very important letter from Keable and Partners, a firm of solicitors. She was discussing the letter with Granny Anne and Grandad Charlie. Then they all went to speak with Aunty Pat and Uncle Jeff. The children noticed that all the adults appeared to be quite pleased and excited about this solicitor's letter.

"What do you think the letter is about?" whispered Amy to the other children.

"No idea" whispered back Wilber." I hope they are going to tell us"

"Me too, me too" whispered Megan and Gemma together.

Suddenly there was a knock at the door. Granny Anne answered the door and there stood a very smart looking young lady carrying a briefcase. The lady was called Miss Dewberry and she was a solicitor.

Mummy called all the children into the house to listen to what Miss Dewberry had to say.

It was very surprising news. .Miss Dewberry told Amy that an old man who had been her father's uncle had died. His name was James Johnson who was married to Meg Johnson who had also died. Miss Dewberry also told Wilber, Megan, Gemma and KC that Meg Johnson was their mother's aunt.

"But what does it all mean?" asked Amy curiously.

"What it means" explained Miss Dewberry " That you Amy are the distant cousin of Wilber, Megan, Gemma and KC.

"WHAT!...REALLY? called out all the shocked children together.

"Yes it is true. We have been searching for you because you five children have been left money in the Will of James and Meg Johnson. The money is to be spent on your education and for when you are older.

"If we are going to be given a lot of money. Can we buy lots of toys and sweets?" Asked KC excitedly..

"Well perhaps you can have a new guitar and some music lessons " said Aunty Pat

"Can I have music lessons too?" asked Wilber eagerly

"Oooh can we have dance lessons?" asked the twins with their toes tapping, hardly able to contain their excitement.

Amy started to think about the wise words that Howard had spoken to her in the Estuary Bookshop. His words about that she was a child of the future; to learn her lesson well and people would enjoy her singing.

"Can I have singing lessons please?" asked Amy "I just want to sing and sing and sing really well."

The adults agreed that the children could have music, dance and singing lessons.

"Hooray" they all shouted out together.

That night in her bedroom, Amy Looked out of her bedroom window. In the distance she could see the towers of the Humber Bridge standing dark, tall and proud against a huge full silvery moon...She stared in wonderment it was just like the night she first saw the Hum Bear.. Amy also thought of her father sailing from Hull on his fishing trawler.

She sat on her bed talking to the Hum Bear. "We have been on an incredible journey together, now everything is starting to work out perfectly. Only you and I have visited the past and the future and have seen what happens. Now is the right time to practise hard on my singing. You have to help me Hum. I have to do as Howard told me. I am a child of the future I need to learn my lesson well so that I may show the way.

"Mmm mmm" murmured the Hum Bear in his usual way.

DID YOU KNOW THESE FACTS ABOUT HULL AND PLACES TO VISIT THAT ARE CONNECTED WITH THE HUM BEAR STORY

Back in 1981 the world's largest single span suspension bridge was opened fulfilling the dreams of many local people. It was called the **Humber Bridge** and it spanned the River Humber between the places of Barton and Hessle close to the **City of Kingston upon Hull.**

Kingston upon Hull is the UK City of Culture of 2017. It is a proud maritime city that is steeped in history. You can learn much of Hull's cultural heritage from many of its fine museums located in the old town.

Hull boasts a spectacular aquarium, **The Deep** which is an award winning visitor's attraction. The Deep is set in a huge dramatic building overlooking the Humber estuary. It is home to thousands of marine life including fish, sharks, rays and penguins. New for 2017 there are live sea turtles as a further addition in the magnificent displays.

Hull has a remarkable art **Fish Trail,** which is a terrific way to explore a two mile route around the historic Old Town. You need to be a very 'eagle eyed explorer' to spot any of the 41 life size sculptures of many different fishes etched along this fascinating route.

Hull as an impressive **Marina** that moors many splendid boats and yachts. The surrounding paved area with appealing café bars and restaurants makes for a very relaxing destination. A short and pleasant walk along the marina takes you to **Victoria Pier.** There are many floral tributes tied on to the pier to honour the many brave and hardworking deep sea fishermen who never returned home from the perils at sea.

Close to The Deep and Marina on the corner of Humber Street is **Dinostar,** Hull's dinosaur museum. Dinostar offers an exciting interactive experience for children of all ages, where you can also hear the dinosaurs roar.

A yearly **Freedom Festival** is held in the centre of Hull, celebrating arts and culture, contributing to the cause of freedom moulded in the spirit of **William Wilberforce,** who was an MP for Hull and campaigned for the abolition of slavery.

In 1734 a large, golden gilded statue of a man on horseback was erected in Low Gate, Market Place, Hull and still stands today. It is affectionately known as '**King Billy**.' It is the statue is of King William the third, William of Orange. Hull was the first city to swear allegiance to the King who was known to them as '*Our Great Deliverer*'

Hull is a very passionate about its football and rugby teams.

Hull Kingston Rovers (HKR) also known as the '***Robins***' who play in red and white team colours. They moved from their long standing home at **Craven Park** in 1989 to the new **KC Lightstream Stadium** on Preston Road in the east side of the city.

In the west side of the city the **KC Stadium** (renamed KCOM Stadium) is home to both **Hull FC rugby team** and **Hull City football team**.

Hull FC's colours are black and white. Their supporter's song is '***Old Faithful***'

Hull City Football Team wear black and amber team colours and are also known as the '***Tigers.***'

Close to the KCOM Stadium in Walton Street a yearly event **Hull Fair**, is held. The kaleidoscope of coloured lights from the vast fairground rides and stalls, shines out brightly over the west Hull area. The Hull Fair is one of the largest travelling fairs in Europe, and has been a great source of enjoyment to generations of families.

Some famous people of Hull connected with the Hum Bear story

Luke Campbell a boxer from Hull won Olympic Gold for Great Britain at the 2012 London Olympic Games. Local telephone provider **KC** commemorated his win by painting gold a telephone box near to St Paul's Boxing Club. The gold telephone box is located in Market Place close to the 'King Billy' statue.

Amy Johnson a fisherman's daughter was born in Hull in 1903. She was an amazing aviator, who became a global super star by being the first woman to fly solo from England to Australia.

A pleasant seating area with pictures and information about Amy Johnson can be seen outside the Prospect Shopping Centre in Hull's Town Centre.

Jean Bishop is a lady in her nineties who dresses in a giant bee costume and collects thousands of pounds for charity. Jean is known as the Bee Lady in her home city of Hull.

Amy and Hum Bear's Route
in Hull's Old Town